THE DEAD MOON

and other tales from
East Anglia and the Fen Country

The DEAD MOON

and other tales from
East Anglia and the
Fen Country

retold by

KEVIN CROSSLEY-HOLLAND

Illustrated by

SHIRLEY FELTS

ANDRE DEUTSCH

First published in 1982 by
André Deutsch Limited
105-106 Great Russell Street, London WC1B 3LJ

First paperback edition published in 1986 by
Faber and Faber

Second paperback edition published 1990 by
André Deutsch Limited

ISBN 0 233 98572 7

Printed in Great Britain by
St Edmundsbury Press, Bury St Edmunds, Suffolk

For Hildegard and Rudi,
Lise, Anne and Johannes Dorner

CONTENTS

The Dead Moon 1

Tom Hickathrift 11

The Suffolk Miracle 21

The Pedlar of Swaffham 27

The Green Mist 39

The Callow Pit Coffer 45

The Dauntless Girl 57

Tiddy Mun 65

The Black Dog of Bungay 73

Yallery Brown 79

The Green Children 87

Sources 97

Glossary 102

The Dead Moon

LONG AGO, the moon used to shine just as she shone last night. And when she shone, she cast her light over the marshland: the great pools of black water, and the creeping trickles of green water, and the squishy mounds that sucked anyone in who stepped on them. She lit up the whole swamp so that people could walk about almost as safely as in broad daylight.

But when the moon did not shine, out came the Things that live in the darkness. They wormed around, waiting for a chance to harm those people who were not safe at home beside their own hearths. Harm and mishap and evil: bogles and dead things and crawling horrors: they all appeared on the nights when the moon did not shine.

The moon came to hear of this. And being kind and good, as she surely is, shining for us night after night instead of going to sleep, she was upset at what was going on behind her back. She said to herself, 'I'll see what's going on for myself. Maybe it's not as bad as people make out.'

And sure enough, at the end of the month the moon stepped down on to the earth, wearing a black cloak and a black hood over her yellow shining hair. She went straight to the edge of the bogland and looked about her.

There was water here, and water there; waving tussocks, trembling mounds, and great black snags of peat all twisted and bent; and in front of her, everything was dark – dark except for the pools glimmering under the stars and the light that came from the moon's own white feet, poking out beneath her black cloak.

The moon walked forward, right into the middle of the marsh, always looking to left and to right, and over her shoulders. Then she saw she had company, and strange company at that.

I

'Witches,' whispered the moon, and the witches grinned at her as they rode past on their huge black cats.

'The eye,' she whispered, and the evil eye glowered at her from the deepest darkness.

'Will-o'-the-wykes,' whispered the moon, and the will-o'-the-wykes danced around her with their lanterns swinging on their backs.

'The dead,' she whispered, and dead folk rose out of the water. Their faces were white and twisted and hell-fire blazed in their empty eye sockets, and they stared blindly around them.

'And dead hands,' whispered the moon. Slimy dripping dead hands slithered about, beckoning and pointing, so cold and wet that they made the moon's skin crawl.

The moon drew her cloak more tightly around her and trembled. But she was resolved not to go back without seeing all there was to be seen. So on she went, stepping as lightly as the summer wind from tuft to tuft between the greedy gurgling water holes.

Just as the moon came up to a big black pool, her foot slipped. With both hands she grabbed at a snag of peat to steady herself, and save herself from tumbling in. But as soon as she touched it, the snag twined itself round her wrists like a pair of handcuffs, and gripped her so that she couldn't escape. The moon pulled and twisted and fought, but it was no good; she was trapped, completely trapped. Then she looked about her, and wondered if anyone at all would be out that night, and pass by, and help her. But she saw nothing except shifting, flurrying evil Things, coming and going, to-ing and fro-ing, all of them busy and all of them up to no good.

After a while, as the moon stood trembling in the dark, she heard something calling in the distance – a voice that called and called, and then died away in a sob. Then the voice was raised again in a screech of pain and fear, and called and called, until the marshes were haunted by that pitiful crying sound. Then the moon heard the sound of steps, someone floundering along, squishing through the mud, slipping on the tufts. And, through the darkness, she saw a pair of hands catching at the snags and tussocks, and a white face with wide, terrified eyes.

It was a man who had strayed into the marsh. The grinning bogles and dead folk and creeping horrors crawled and crowded around him; voices mocked him; the dead hands plucked at him. And, ahead of him, the will-o'-the-wykes dangled their lanterns, and shook with glee as they lured him further and further away from the safe path over the swamp. Trembling with fear and loathing at the Things all around him, the man struggled on towards the flickering lights ahead of him that looked as if they would give him help and bring him home in safety.

'You over there!' yelled the man. 'You! I'm caught in the swamp. Can you hear me?' His voice rose to a shriek. 'Help! You over there! Help! God and Mary save me from these horrors.' Then the man paused, and sobbed and moaned, and called on the saints and wise women and on God Himself to save him from the swamp.

But then the man shrieked again as the slimy slithery Things crawled around him and reared up so that he could not even see the false lights, the will-o'-the-wykes, ahead of him.

As if matters were not bad enough already, the horrors began to take on all sorts of shapes: beautiful girls winked at him with their bright eyes, and stretched out soft helping hands towards him. But when he tried to catch hold of them, they changed in his grip to slimy things and shapeless worms, and evil voices derided him and mocked him with foul laughter. Then all the bad thoughts that the man had ever had, and all the bad things that he had ever done, came and whispered in his ears, and danced about, and shouted out all the secrets that were buried in his own heart. The man shrieked and sobbed with pain and with shame, and the horrors crawled and gibbered around him and mocked him.

When the poor moon saw that the man was getting nearer and nearer to the deep water holes and deadly sinking mud, and further and further from firm ground, she was so angry and so sorry for him that she struggled and fought and pulled harder than ever. She still couldn't break loose. But with all her twisting and tugging, her black hood fell back from her shining yellow hair. And the beautiful light that came from it drove away the darkness.

The man cried for joy to see God's own light again. And at once the evil Things, unable to stand the light, scurried and delved and dropped away into their dark corners. They left the man and fled.

And the man could see where he was, and where the path was, and which way to take to get out of the marsh.

He was in such a hurry to get away from the sinking mud and the swamp, and all the Things that lived there, that he scarcely glanced at the brave light that shone from the beautiful shining yellow hair streaming out over the black cloak, and falling into the water at his very feet.

And the moon herself was so taken up with saving the man, and so happy that he was back on the right path, that she completely forgot she needed help herself. For she was still trapped in the clutches of the black snag.

The man made off, gasping and stumbling and exhausted, sobbing for joy, running for his life out of the terrible swamp. Then the moon realised how much she would have liked to go with him. She shook with terror. And she pulled and fought as if she were mad, until, worn out with tugging, she fell to her knees at the foot of the snag. As the moon lay there, panting, the black hood fell forward over her head. And although she tried to toss it back again, it caught in her hair and would not move.

Out went that beautiful light, and back came the darkness with all its evil creatures, screeching and howling. They crowded around the moon, mocking at her and snatching at her and striking her; shrieking with rage and spite; swearing with foul mouths, spitting and snarling. They knew she was their old enemy, the brave bright moon, who drove them back into their corners and stopped them from doing all their wicked deeds. They swarmed all around her and made a ghastly clapperdatch. The poor moon crouched in the mud, trembling and sick at heart, and wondered when they would make an end of their caterwauling, and an end of her.

'Damn you!' yelled the witches. 'You've spoiled our spells all this last year.'

'And you keep us in our narrow coffins at night,' moaned the dead folk.

'And you send us off to skulk in the corners,' howled the bogles.

Then all the Things shouted in one voice, 'Ho, ho! Ho, ho!'

The tussocks shook and the water gurgled and the Things raised their voices again.

'We'll poison her – poison her!' shrieked the witches.

'Ho, ho!' howled the Things again.

'We'll smother her – smother her!' whispered the crawling horrors, and they twined themselves around her knees.

'Ho, ho!' shouted all the rest of them.

'We'll strangle her – strangle her!' screeched the dead hands, and they plucked at her throat with cold fingers.

'Ho, ho!' they all yelled again.

And the dead folk writhed and grinned all around her, and chuckled to themselves. 'We'll bury you – bury you down with us in the black earth!'

Once more they all shouted, full of spite and ill will. The poor moon crouched low, and wished she were dead and done for.

The Things of the darkness fought and squabbled over what should be done with the moon until the sky in the east paled and turned grey; it drew near to dawn. When they saw that, they were all worried that they would not have time to do their worst. They caught hold of the moon with horrid bony fingers, and laid her deep in the water at the foot of the snag.

The dead folk held her down while the bogles found a strange big stone. They rolled it right on top of her to stop her from getting up again.

Then the Things told two will-o'-the-wykes to take turns at standing on the black snag to watch over the moon and make sure she lay safe and still. They didn't want her to get away and spoil their sport with her light, or help the poor marshmen at night to avoid the sinking mud and the water holes.

Then, as the grey light began to brighten, the shapeless Things fled into their dark corners; the dead folk crept back into the water, or crammed themselves into their coffins; and the witches went home to work their spells and curses. And the green slimy water shone in the light of dawn as if nothing, no wicked or evil creature, had ever gone near it.

There lay the poor moon, dead and buried in the marsh, until someone would set her free. And who knew even where to look for her?

✻   ✻   ✻

Days passed, nights passed, and it was time for the birth of the new moon. People put pennies in their pockets, and straw in their caps, so as to be ready for it. They looked up at the sky uneasily, for the moon was a good friend to the marsh folk, and they were only too happy when she began to wax, and the pathways were safe again, and the evil Things were driven back by her blessed light into the darkness and the water holes.

But day followed day and the new moon never rose. The nights were always dark and the evil Things were worse than ever. It was not safe at all to travel alone, and the boggarts crept and wailed round the houses of the marsh folk. They peeped through the windows and tipped the latches until the poor people had to burn candles and lamps all night to stop the horrors from crossing their thresholds and forcing their way in.

The bogles and other creatures seemed to have lost all their fear. They howled and laughed and screeched around the hamlet, as if they were trying to wake the dead themselves. The marsh folk listened, and sat trembling and shaking by their fires. They couldn't sleep or rest or put a foot out of doors, and one dark and dreary night followed another.

When days turned into weeks and the new moon still did not rise, the villagers were upset and afraid. A group of them went to the wise woman who lived in the old mill, and asked her if she could find out where the moon had gone.

The wise woman looked in the cauldron, and in the mirror, and in the Book. 'Well,' she said, 'it's queer. I can't tell you for sure what has happened to her.'

She shook her head and the marsh folk shook their heads.

'It's only dark, dead,' said the wise woman. 'You must wait a while, and let me think about it, and then maybe I'll be able to help you. If you hear of anything, any clue, come by and tell me. And,' said the wise woman, 'be sure to put a pinch of salt, a straw and a button on the doorstep each night. The horrors will never cross it then, light or no light.'

Then the marsh folk left the wise woman and the mill and went their separate ways. As the days went by, and the new moon never rose, they talked and talked. They wondered and pondered and worried and guessed, at home and in the inn and in the fields around the marshland.

One day, sitting on the great settle in the inn, a group of men were discussing the whereabouts of the moon, and another customer, a man from the far end of the marshland, smoked and listened to the talk. Suddenly this stranger sat up and slapped his knee. 'My Lord!' he said. 'I'd clean forgotten, but I reckon I know where the moon is.'

All the men sitting on the settle turned round to look at him. Then the stranger told them about how he had got lost in the marsh and how, when he was almost dead with fright, the light had shone out, and all the evil Things fled from it, and he had found the marsh-path and got home safely.

'And I was so terrified,' said the stranger, 'that I didn't really look to see where the light had come from. But I do remember it was white and soft like the moon herself.

'And **this light** came from something dark,' said the man, 'standing near a black snag in the water.' He paused and puffed at his pipe. 'I didn't really look,' he said again, 'but I think I remember a shining face and yellow hair in the middle of the dazzle. It had a sort of kind look, like the old moon herself above the marshland at night.'

At once all the men got up from the settle and went back to the wise woman. They told her everything the stranger had said. She listened and then stared once more, stared long into the cauldron and into the Book. Then she nodded. 'It's still dark,' she said, 'and I can't see anything for sure. But do as I tell you, and you can find out for yourselves. All of you must meet just before night falls. Put a stone in your mouths,' said the wise woman, 'and take a hazel twig in your hands, and say never a word until you're safe home again. Then step out and fear nothing! Make your way into the middle of the marsh, until you find a coffin, a candle and a cross.' The wise woman stared at the circle of anxious faces around her. 'Then you won't be far from your moon,' she said. 'Search, and maybe you'll find her.'

The men looked at each other and scratched their heads.

'But where will we find her, mother?' asked one.

'And which of us must go?' asked another.

'And the bogles, won't they do for us?' said a third.

'Houts!' exclaimed the wise woman impatiently. 'You parcel of fools! I can tell you no more. Do as I've told you and fear nothing.' She glared at the men. 'And if you don't like my advice, stay at home. Do without your moon if that's what you want.'

The next day, at dusk, all the men in the hamlet came out of their houses. Each had a stone in his mouth and a hazel twig in his hand, and each was feeling nervous and creepy.

Then the men stumbled and stuttered along the paths out into the middle of the marsh. It was so dark that they could see almost nothing. But they heard sighings and flusterings, and they could feel wet fingers touching them. On they went, peering about for the coffin, the candle and the cross, until they came near to the pool next to the great snag where the moon lay buried.

All at once they stopped in their tracks, quaking and shaking and scared. For there they saw the great stone, half in and half out of the water, looking for all the world like a strange big coffin. And at its head stood the black snag, stretching out its two arms in a dark gruesome cross. A little light flickered on it, like a dying candle.

The men knelt down in the mud, and crossed themselves, and said the Lord's Prayer to themselves. First they said it forwards because of the cross, and then they said it backwards, to keep the bogles away. But they mouthed it all without so much as a whisper, for they knew the evil Things would catch them if they did not do as the wise woman had told them.

Then the men shuffled to the edge of the water. They took hold of the big stone, and levered it up, and for one moment, just one moment, they saw a strange and beautiful face looking up at them, and looking so grateful, out of the black water.

But then the light came so quickly, and was so white and shining, that the men stepped back, stunned by it, and by the great angry wail raised by the fleeing horrors. And the very next minute, when they came to their senses, the men saw the full moon in the sky. She was as bright and beautiful and kind as ever, shining and smiling down at them; she showed the marsh and the marsh-paths as clearly as daylight and stole into every nook and cranny, as though she would have liked to drive the darkness and the bogles away for ever.

Then the marsh folk went home with light hearts and happy. And, ever since, the moon has shone more brightly and clearly over the marshland than anywhere else.

Tom Hickathrift

⸺◈⸺

BEFORE THE REIGN OF William the Conqueror, there lived in the marshes of the Isle of Ely a man whose name was Thomas Hickathrift. He was a poor man, a labourer, but very strong and able to do two days' work in one. He called his one son by his own name, Thomas, and sent him to a good school. But Tom was none too clever; indeed, he was a bit soft in the head, and would not apply himself, so he learned nothing.

When Thomas Hickathrift died, Tom's mother went out to work. She loved her son dearly, and supported him as best she could. But Tom himself was so slothful that he would not turn his hand at anything, let alone do a good day's work. He liked nothing so much as to loaf in the chimney corner, and ate as much at one sitting as would four or five normal men.

When he was only ten years old, Tom was eight foot tall; he measured sixty inches round the waist and his hand was like a shoulder of mutton. There was no part of him that was not outsize.

One day, Tom's poor mother went to ask her neighbour, a rich farmer, if he could spare her a bundle of straw.

'Take as much as you want,' said the farmer, who was an honest, charitable man.

Tom's mother hurried home and said to her son, 'Will you go up to the farm and fetch me a bundle of straw?'

'Damn it!' said Tom. 'Let me be.'

'No,' said Tom's old mother. 'Please go.'

'I'll only go,' said Tom, 'if you can borrow a cart rope for me.'

Tom's mother needed the straw, and saw she would not get it without humouring her son. So she went off to another neighbour and borrowed a cart rope.

Then Tom got out of the chimney corner, took the rope, and walked up to the farm. He found the farmer in the barn, watching two farmhands thresh the corn. 'My mother has told me to come up for a bundle of straw,' he said.

'Take as much as you can carry, Tom,' said the farmer.

Tom stretched out the rope on the barn floor, and laid the straw along it – armful after armful.

'If you go on like that,' said one farmhand, 'your rope will be too short to go round it.'

The farmer and the other lad shook their heads at Tom's stupidity, but Tom took no notice. He gathered more straw, and then drew the rope round it all.

'That will weigh a ton,' said the farmer. 'Twenty hundredweight.'

'You won't be able to carry that,' said one lad.

'What a fool!' jeered the other.

By way of answer, Tom lifted the bundle and swung it on to his shoulder. He made no more of it than if it had weighed a single hundredweight and, turning his back on the farmer and his two lads, he strode out of the barn.

When Tom's strength became known, his neighbours gave him no rest. Nobody would let him go on basking by the fire and everybody wanted to hire him to do this job and that job. Seeing that he was so strong, they told him it was a disgrace that he should lead such a lazy life, and do nothing from day to day.

Tom became so tired of this baiting and taunting that he set to work, disposing of one job after another. Then, one day, a man came to Tom's house and asked him to help bring back a tree trunk from a nearby wood.

Tom agreed to help, and the man hired four other lads besides. When they reached the fallen tree in the wood, the man and the lads placed the cart alongside it and tried to hoist it with pulleys. But they were unable to move the tree one inch.

'Stand back, you fools!' said Tom. He bent down, and lifted the trunk so that it stood on one end. Then he laid it on the cart.

'There!' said Tom. 'There's a man's work for you.'

'It is and all,' said the man, marvelling.

Just as they were coming out of the wood, Tom and his companions met the forester and exchanged greetings. 'Can you spare a stick,' asked Tom, 'for my old mother's fire?'

'Of course,' said the forester. 'Take whatever you can carry.'

Tom looked round and saw another fallen tree, even larger than the one lying in the cart. He humped it on to one shoulder, and then he walked home with it as fast as six horses could have drawn it on the cart.

When Tom realised that he had more strength than twenty men, he began to enjoy himself. For the first time in his life, he made good friends with other lads. He ran races against them, and held jumping contests and, delighting in their company, went with them to fairs and meetings to see the sports and other amusements.

Tom once went to a fair that had attracted every lad in the district – some went to cudgel, some to wrestle, some to throw the hammer. For a time Tom stood and watched this sport and that sport, and then he approached a group of young men who were throwing the hammer.

'Here's a manlike sport,' said Tom.

'It is,' said the young men. 'Do you want to try your hand?'

Tom took the hammer in one hand and tried it for weight. 'Stand out of the way, then,' said Tom.

'Yes, yes,' said the blacksmith.

'Stand out of the way!' said Tom. 'I'm going to throw it as far as I can.'

'Yes, yes, Tom,' jeered the blacksmith, winking at his friends. 'I'm sure you'll be able to throw it a great distance.'

Tom grasped the hammer and threw it. It soared through the air and fell smack into a river more than a thousand yards off.

'Yes, yes,' said Tom to the blacksmith, smiling. 'Now you can go and fetch your hammer.'

After Tom had shown his strength at throwing the hammer, he thought he would try his hand at wrestling. He had no more skill than an ass, and all that he did, he did by brute force. Yet he threw everyone who stood against him – they were done for as soon as Tom took a grip on them. Some opponents he threw over his head, some he spread-eagled at his feet. He never engaged in clinches and never tripped anyone; he simply picked them up and hurled them two or three yards, so that they were in danger of breaking their necks. Before long, there was nobody left who was ready to climb into the ring with Tom. They all took him to be some devil come amongst them; and Tom's fame spread more widely than ever.

Tom took such delight in sport that he would travel near or far to any fair or festival that promised cudgel-play or bear-baiting or a game of football. So when he was out riding one day in a part of the country where he was a stranger, and happened to come across a group of lads who were playing football for a wager, Tom dismounted at once and watched the game for a while.

One of the players miskicked the ball and it bounced towards Tom. Tom swung a leg and gave the ball such a boot that the players saw it fly through the air, and no one could tell how far it had gone and where it had come to ground. They were unable to find their ball again and their game was ruined.

First the players were astonished, and then they rounded on Tom and called him a wrecker.

Tom said nothing. He walked across to a nearby house that had collapsed in a recent storm, picked up a beam, and began to lay about him. All those that got in the way he either killed or stunned. The whole district was up in arms against Tom, but it was all in vain; no one was able to stand up to him.

It was quite late that evening before Tom made his way home. On the road, he met four thieves notorious for robbing people who passed that way. No one could escape them, and they robbed everyone they came across, both rich and poor.

When they saw Tom, alone as he was, they thought that he would be easy prey, and they would soon have his money. They were mistaken; it was the other way round!

'Stand and deliver!' shouted the thieves.

'What?' said Tom. 'What should I deliver?'

'Your money, sir,' they said.

'My money,' said Tom. 'First you must ask for it better; and second, you must be better armed.'

'Come,' said the men. 'We're not here to gossip. We're here for your money, and your money we'll have before you move from this place.'

'Really?' said Tom. 'Is that really so? Well, then, you must come and get it.'

One of the thieves thrust at Tom but Tom grabbed his sword, which was made of trusty steel, and struck so fiercely at the others that they were afraid for their lives, and spurred their horses. Tom was not having that. Seeing that one of the thieves was carrying a portmanteau behind him, and rightly taking it to be stuffed with money, Tom redoubled his efforts. He killed two of the thieves and wounded the other two so grievously that they begged for mercy. Tom spared their lives but took all their money – two hundred pounds in all – to sweeten his journey home.

The next day, when Tom was walking through the forest near his home, he met a brawny tinker who had a good strong staff over one shoulder and a large dog who was carrying his bag and tools.

'Where are you from?' asked Tom. 'And where are you going? There's no highway here.'

'What's that to me?' said the tinker. 'Mind your own business! Only fools are meddlers.'

'What's that for me?' roared Tom. 'I'll help you to understand, before we part company, what it is to me.' And with that, he put his fist in front of the tinker's nose.

'All right,' said the tinker. 'It's three long years now since I had a scrap. I've challenged countless men but nobody dares take me on. As far as I can see, this whole county is full of nothing but cowards.' The tinker grinned. 'Though I have heard,' he added, 'that there's a strong lad hereabouts called Tom Hickathrift. I'd like to meet him, all right. I'd like to have a turn with him.'

'Yes,' said Tom, 'and he might well get the better of you. Here he is. You've met him.'

'What?' said the tinker.

'I am he,' said Tom. 'Now what do you say?'

'Why,' cried the tinker, 'I'm delighted that we've met, if only by accident. Now we can try our strength on each other.'

'Is this a joke,' asked Tom, 'or are you serious?'

'No,' said the tinker, 'and yes, I'm in earnest.'

'All right!' said Tom. 'Let me get a twig first.'

'Of course,' said the tinker. 'Hang the man who fights an un-armed man! I've got no time for that.'

So Tom stepped over to the nearby gate and wrenched off the diagonal bar for a staff. Then they started fighting; the tinker thrust at Tom and Tom thrust at the tinker. They fought with the strength of two giants. The tinker was wearing a leather coat and every time Tom struck him the coat screeched, but for all that the tinker didn't give Tom an inch.

But then Tom gave the tinker a blow on the side of his head that felled him. 'Now, tinker,' said Tom, 'now where are you?'

But the tinker was nimble. He leaped up again and struck Tom with his staff so that Tom staggered sideways; the tinker rained blow after blow on Tom, and then swiped at his head from the other side so that Tom's neck cracked with the strain.

Tom threw down his weapon. 'You're a match for me, tinker, and more than a match,' he said. 'Come home with me now.' So he took the tinker home to recover from his wounds and bruises, and from that day onward, they were the best of friends.

Tom's fame spread far and wide, and came to the ears of a brewer in King's Lynn who needed a good strong man to carry his beer across the marshes to Wisbech.

Tom was not eager to work for him, but the brewer begged him, and offered him a new suit of clothes from top to toe, and as much good food and drink as he desired. So Tom at last agreed to work for the brewer, and the brewer told him exactly which way to go. For there was a monstrous giant who ranged over part of the marsh, and nobody dared go near him. Those who did, he either killed or used as his servants.

Tom did more work in one day than all the other men employed by the brewer did in three. The brewer was delighted, and made Tom his chief assistant; every day Tom took the beer alone to Wisbech and a long way it was – twenty miles along the road that skirted the marsh and twenty miles back again.

Tom found the journey wearisome and realised that the quickest way to Wisbech, over the land controlled by the giant, would be less than half the distance. Eating so well and drinking so much strong ale day after day, Tom was half as powerful again as he had been before; and so, one morning, without saying anything to the brewer or his fellow servants, he decided to go to Wisbech by the quicker route, or else lose his life – to win the horse, as people say, or lose the saddle.

Tom drove his horses and cart and flung open the gates that led to the path over the marsh. It wasn't long before the giant spied Tom and stormed up to him, intending to seize all his beer as a prize. He greeted Tom like a lion, as though he meaned to devour him. 'Who gave you the right to come this way?' he roared. 'Haven't you heard that everyone is afraid of the sight of me? How dare you fling open the gates to my land just as you please?'

Tom stood there and said nothing. He didn't give a fart for the giant.

'Have you no thought for your life?' asked the giant. 'I'll make an example of you for all the other rogues under the sun. You see how many heads are hanging on that tree over there, the heads of men who have trespassed against me? Your head will hang higher than all the rest.'

'A turd in your teeth!' said Tom. 'You won't find that I'm quite the same as them.'

'No?' said the giant. 'You're nothing but a fool. What do you think you're doing, coming to fight against me? You haven't even got a weapon.'

'I have a weapon here,' said Tom, 'that will show you up for a rogue and a coward.'

'Right!' said the giant, and he ran into his cave to fetch his great club, meaning to dash out Tom's brains with the first blow.

Now Tom did not know what to do for a weapon, for he saw that his whip would be little use against the giant who was twelve foot tall and six foot round the waist. But while the giant was getting his club, he had a good idea. He overturned his cart, and took one wheel and the axletree for shield and buckler.

The giant came out of his cave and stared at Tom, amazed to see him holding the wheel in one hand and the axletree in the other. 'You're going to do a great job with those weapons,' he bawled.

'I've got a twig here that will beat you and your wheel and axletree into the ground.' The giant's twig was as thick as a mill post but Tom was not afraid. He saw there was nothing for it but to kill or be killed.

Then the giant struck at Tom with his club. Tom parried the blow with his shield and the rim of the wheel cracked. But Tom, meanwhile, struck at the giant with his axletree. He hit the giant on the side of his head and made him reel. 'What?' said Tom, 'Are you drunk on my strong beer already?'

The giant recovered and rained blows on Tom. But Tom parried them all with his wheel so that he was not hurt at all. And he in turn struck such savage blows that sweat and blood streamed down the giant's face. Being fat and foggy and almost exhausted by the long fight, the giant asked Tom, 'Let me drink a little. Then we'll fight again.'

'No, no,' said Tom. 'I never learned enough from my mother to be such a fool.' Tom saw that the giant was beginning to weary, and that his blows were becoming weaker, and thought it was best to make hay while the sun shone. He assaulted the giant with one blow after another until at last he felled him.

The giant roared and bawled and begged Tom not to kill him. He offered to do anything for Tom, and even to be his servant. But Tom had no more mercy on him than on a bear cub. He went on hitting him until he was dead and then he cut off the giant's head.

Then Tom went into the giant's cave and looked around. He found such a store of gold and silver that his heart leaped at the sight of it. After a while, however, he left it all as it was and calmly resumed his journey to Wisbech, where he delivered the beer just as usual.

When Tom got home, he told his master, the brewer, all that had happened. The brewer was overjoyed but could scarcely believe his ears. 'Seeing is believing,' he said. 'Seeing is believing.'

So the next day Tom and his master and most of the townsfolk of King's Lynn went out into the marsh. They came to the place where Tom had met the giant, and there Tom showed them the head, and the gold and silver in the cave. They all laughed and leaped for joy, for the giant had been a great terror and threat to them all.

The news of how Tom Hickathrift had killed a giant spread up and down the country. Many people came to see the dead giant and his cave; everyone lit bonfires; and Tom was even more respected than before.

By common consent, Tom took possession of the cave and its contents, and everyone said that he deserved twice as much. Tom pulled down the cave and, with the rocks, built a fine house on the same site. Some of the land that the giant had seized Tom gave to the poor as common land; and the rest he divided into fields, and grew crops, to support himself and his old mother, Jane Hickathrift.

Tom had won a name far and wide and became the most influential man in the district. People called him Mr Hickathrift, and feared his anger just as much as they had feared the giant before. He had manservants and maidservants, he made a deer park, and erected a church dedicated to St James, because he had killed the giant on that saint's feast day. So Tom lived a fine and happy life, visited now and then by his friend the tinker, until the end of his days.

The Suffolk Miracle

THERE WAS ONCE a rich farmer in Suffolk. When he stood in the middle of his land, he could see nothing that he did not own – fields of swaying corn and silken barley, a copse of pale ash trees, his farm and its outbuildings, hayricks and horses and all his farm machinery.

But much as he cared about his crops, the farmer cared much more for his daughter, Rosamund. With her pools of dark eyes and oval white face and waterfall of jet-black hair, she was as beautiful as any girl in the county. As she grew up, she was her parents' delight in all that she thought and said and did.

But then Frank, the ploughboy, fell in love with Rosamund. Rosamund's eye brightened and her cheek flushed and she walked about with an inner smile. It was as if she were bewitched by him.

The farmer did not see things in this way. He thought no good could come of a match between a rich farmer's daughter and a poor ploughboy, and said as much to Rosamund.

Rosamund took no notice. In the early evenings, when the day's work was done, she spirited herself out of the farm and away into the cornfields and her lover's arms.

The farmer and his wife decided to put an end to this business once and for all. Despite her protests and tears, and despite the thorn in their own hearts, they sent Rosamund away to stay with her uncle – the farmer's brother – forty miles away.

'There you'll go,' said her father.

'No,' cried Rosamund.

'. . . and there you'll remain until you've forgotten about this Frank.'

Frank could plough a straight furrow across a field; he could plough a whole field fair and square. But he was not a talker, he let the things he did speak for him.

When he was cut off from his Rosamund, Frank said even less. He was inconsolable. He left the farmer's service and took to walking all day by himself. He walked for mile after mile across the shining fields and along the green lanes of Suffolk. And if he talked at all, he talked to the birds and wild animals, and talked to the wind.

Frank grew wan and thin; he took less and less pleasure in the breathing world around him; he lived in a dream and his dream was of Rosamund.

It was as if Frank were cut off from the spring from which his own life flowed. He took to his bed. Did he even listen to what the doctor prescribed? Did he even hear all that his family and friends said? It was no good. Frank the ploughboy was sick of love; he was incurable, and he died.

'Better not tell her,' said the farmer to his wife. 'Let her get over Frank in her own good time.'

Although she was cut off from Frank, Rosamund did not give up hope. 'Love is stronger than time,' she said to herself, and thought that in time things might change: either her parents would relent, or Frank would make his fortune, or something would happen.

One evening, about a month after Frank's death, Rosamund and her uncle were sitting in front of the fire when there was a tap on the door.

'Very late,' said her uncle, frowning.

Rosamund got up and drew back the bolt and opened the door.

'Frank!' she cried. 'Oh Frank, it's you!' Rosamund threw herself into her lover's arms.

'Rosamund,' said Frank, 'You're to come home with me. That's what your parents say.'

'Praise be to God!' cried Rosamund. 'I knew they would, I knew they would. And I will come home with you.'

Rosamund's uncle got up from the fire and joined them.

'Uncle,' cried Rosamund, 'this is Frank and he's come for me and I'm to go home with him.'

'I hoped as much,' said her uncle, smiling.

'Look!' said Rosamund. 'My father's best horse! My mother's hood!'

'Proof,' said Frank.

'As if I need proof,' said Rosamund.

'Yes, I hoped it would come to this,' said Rosamund's uncle. 'True lovers never can be parted.'

Rosamund kissed her uncle goodbye and mounted behind Frank. They galloped out of the courtyard, and the horse's hooves struck sparks from the paving-stones. Rosamund put her arms round her lover's waist and they rode into the darkness.

'My head aches,' said Frank.

Then Rosamund pulled out her white handkerchief and tied it round Frank's forehead. 'My!' she said. 'Your forehead's cold. It's as cold as clay. We'll have a fire when we get home.'

Within two hours, Rosamund and Frank had covered forty miles and were back at her father's farm. Rosamund dismounted and patted the horse's steaming flank.

'You go in,' said Frank. 'I'll put the horse into the stable.'

Rosamund walked to the door and tried it; it was locked. So she went round the house and tried the kitchen door, and that was locked too. Then she rapped sharply, surprised that there were no lights burning upstairs or downstairs, and no one to welcome her. Rosamund shivered under the stars and rapped again more loudly. At last there was a scuffling and a scrabbling inside and a voice called out, 'Who's there?'

'Rosamund.'

'Who?' said the voice.

'It's me, Rosamund.'

'Wait!' said the voice.

Rosamund frowned, and for a while there was silence. The owner of the voice, a sleepy farmhand, went upstairs and woke the farmer; and the farmer came stumbling downstairs in his nightshirt and unbolted the door.

'Father!' cried Rosamund.

'You!' said the farmer, astonished. 'How did you get here?'

'How . . . what do you mean?' faltered Rosamund.

'How did you get here?' repeated the farmer.

'Didn't you send for me,' said Rosamund gaily, 'and with your own horse? Frank came and collected me just two hours ago.'

'Frank . . .' echoed her father, and the word died on his lips.

'He's got so cold,' said Rosamund, 'as cold as clay. I had to tie my handkerchief round his forehead.'

'Where is he then?' said the farmer quietly.

'In the stable,' said Rosamund.

'You go in,' said her father, 'and get ready for bed. I'll make sure the horse is well littered.'

Rosamund frowned and shook her head and stepped into the farmhouse; its warmth seeped into her and made her feel utterly weary.

The farmer, meanwhile, walked out in his nightshirt and hurried round to the stable. Then he raised his candle and peered about. There was no one there, and not a sound but one horse munching.

The farmer looked into each stall and saw that his best horse was sweating all over. Then the farmer shivered, and not because he was only wearing a nightshirt.

Slowly he made his way back to the house and slowly he walked upstairs to his daughter's room.

'So much to say,' said Rosamund sleepily. 'So good to be home again.'

'In the morning,' said the farmer gently. 'It's late now. You'll see him in the morning.'

The farmer did not sleep, not for one minute. He lay on his bed, and tossed, and got up and dressed at first light. Then he walked round his farm, wondering what to do, and everything looked ashen. An hour passed and the day quickened. The farmer went back to the house and up to Rosamund's room. He woke her just as the sun broke the eastern horizon and flooded her bedroom with its yellow light.

'Father,' sighed Rosamund. 'I knew you would.'

The farmer sat down on the end of his daughter's bed. 'Rosamund,' he said, 'I must tell you now: Frank is dead.'

Rosamund sat up, her dark eyes wide and terrified.

'. . . and he died one month ago. Your mother and I, we thought it best not to tell you.'

'It isn't true,' cried Rosamund. 'You know I rode with him last night, he brought me home to you.'

It was just as the farmer feared; nothing that he said began to convince his daughter that Frank lay dead. He shook his head, unhappy at her distress, unhappy at the thought that Frank's ghost might be walking.

'It *is* true,' said the farmer, 'and we'll have to prove it.'

When Rosamund was dressed, she and her father went down to the little cottage where Frank's old father lived.

'One month ago now,' he said sadly, and looked at the ground.

'It isn't true what you say,' cried Rosamund wildly. 'Why are you trying to hide him from me?'

'After last night, she won't believe it,' said the farmer.

'True love never dies,' said Frank's father.

'That's as maybe,' said the farmer sourly.

'Well, there's only one way to settle it,' said Frank's father.

'That's what I was thinking,' said the farmer. 'And settle it we must, or your son will go on walking and my daughter will go mad.'

The three of them found the sexton in the graveyard. They told him what had happened during the night and the sexton agreed to dig up Frank's grave. He dug and dug until he was waist-deep in the ground. Then he unearthed Frank's coffin and, as Rosamund and the two men stared down, he brushed away the earth and prised open the lid.

There lay Frank, one month dead, his body already turning into mould.

Rosamund screamed.

There lay Frank, one month dead, his body already turning into mould; and he had a white handkerchief tied round his forehead.

Rosamund toppled and crumpled into the grave. She was taken back to the farm, and nursed night and day, but she never recovered. No, it was not long before the two lovers lay side by side, sleeping cold in the churchyard.

The Pedlar of Swaffham

ONE NIGHT John Chapman had a dream.

A man stood by him, dressed in a surcoat as red as blood; and the man said, 'Go to London Bridge. Go and be quick. Go, good will come of it.'

John the pedlar woke with a start. 'Cateryne,' he whispered, 'Cateryne, wake up! I've had a dream.'

Cateryne, his wife, groaned and tossed and turned. 'What?' she said.

'I've had a dream.'

'Go to sleep, John,' she said; and she fell asleep again.

John lay and wondered at his dream; and while he lay wondering he too fell asleep. But the man in scarlet came a second time, and said, 'Go to London Bridge. Go and be quick. Go, good will come of it.'

The pedlar sat up in the dark. 'Cateryne!' he growled. 'Wake up! Wake up! I've had the same dream again.'

Cateryne groaned and tossed and turned. 'What?' she said.

Then John told her his dream.

'You,' she said, 'you would believe anything.'

The moment he woké next morning, the pedlar of Swaffham remembered his dream. He told it to his children, Margaret and Hue and Dominic. He told it to his wife again.

'Forget it!' said Cateryne.

So John went about his business as usual and, as usual, his mastiff went with him. He fed his pig and hens in the back yard. He hoisted his pack on his broad shoulders and went to the market place; he set up his stall of pots and pans, household goods of one kind and another, phials and potions, special trimmings for ladies' gowns. He gossiped with his friends – the butcher, the baker, the smith, the shoemaker and the weaver, the dyer and many another. But no matter what he did, the pedlar could not escape his dream. He shook his lion-head, he rubbed his blue eyes, but the dream seemed real and everything else seemed dreamlike. 'What am I to do?' he said.

And his mastiff opened his jaws, and yawned.

That evening John Chapman walked across the market place to the tumbledown church. And there he found the thin priest, Master Fuller; his holy cheekbones shone in the half-light. 'Well, what is it?' Master Fuller said.

Then John told him about his strange dream.

'I dream, you dream, everyone dreams,' said the priest impatiently, swatting dust from his black gown. 'Dream of how we can get gold to rebuild our church! This ramshackle place is an insult to God.'

The two of them stood and stared sadly about them: all the walls of stone were rickety and uneven; the roof of the north aisle had fallen in, and through it they could see the crooked spire.

John Chapman gave a long sigh. 'Gold,' he said. 'I wish I could.'

Then the pedlar left the church and went back to his small cottage. But he was still uneasy. Nothing he did, and nothing anyone had said, seemed to make any difference; he could not forget his dream.

That night Cateryne said, 'You've talked and talked of the man with the surcoat as red as blood. You've been more dreaming than awake. Perhaps, after all, you must go to London Bridge.'

'I'll go,' said John. 'I'll go and be quick.'

Next day, John Chapman got up at first light. At once he began to make ready for his journey. He hurried about, he banged his head against a beam, his face turned red. 'I must take five gold pieces,' he said. 'I must take my cudgel.'

'You must take your hood,' said Cateryne.

Then John looked at his mastiff. 'I must take you,' he said. And the mastiff thumped the ground with his tail; dust and chaff flew through the air.

'Tell no one where I've gone,' said John Chapman. 'I don't want to be the laughing-stock of Swaffham.'

Then, while the pedlar ate his fill of meat and curds, Cateryne put more food into his pack – cheese, and two loaves made of beans and bran, and a gourd full of ale.

So everything was ready. And just as the June sun rose behind a light cloud, a great coin of gold, John kissed his wife and his children good-bye.

'Come back,' called little Dominic.

They stood by the door, the four of them, waving and waving until the pedlar with his pack, his cudgel and his mastiff, had walked out of Swaffham; out of sight.

John Chapman strode past the archery butts just outside the town; he hurried between fields white with sheep. At first he knew the way well, but then the rough highway that men called the Gold Road left the open fields behind and passed through sandy heathland where there were no people, no sheep, no villages.

Soon the rain came, heavy, blurring everything. John pulled his hood over his head, but the water seeped through it. It soaked through his clothes, dripped from his nose.

By midday, he was tired and steaming. So he stopped to eat food and give a bone to his mastiff. And while they ate, some lord's messenger, decked out in red and blue, galloped by and spattered them with mud.

'The devil take him!' the pedlar said.

During the afternoon, the rain eased and the pedlar and his dog were able to quicken their pace. They made good progress; one by one, the milestones dropped away.

But that evening it grew dark before the pedlar could find any shelter, even a peasant's shack or some deserted hovel. John had no choice but to sleep in the open, under an oak tree. 'God help us,' he said, 'if there are wolves.'

But there were no wolves, only strange nightsounds: the tree groaning and creaking, wind in the moaning leaves and wind in the rustling grass, the barking of fox and vixen. When first light came, John could barely get to his feet for the ache in his cold bones and the cramp in his empty stomach.

And his mastiff hobbled about as if he were a hundred.

So for four days they walked on. Every hour contained its own surprise; John talked to a friendly priest who had been to Jerusalem; he walked with a couple of vagabonds who wanted him to go to a fair at Waltham; he shook off a rascally pardoner who tried to sell him a ticket to heaven; he saw rabbits, and hares, and deer; he gazed down from hill-crests at tapestries of fields; he followed the way through dark forests where only silence lived. Never in his life had John seen so many strangers nor set eyes on so many strange things. He said to his mastiff, 'We're foreigners in our own country.'

Sometimes the pedlar's pack chafed at his shoulders; often he envied the many travellers with horses – pilgrims and merchants, scholars and monks; but not for one moment did he forget his purpose. For as long as it was light, John Chapman made haste, following the Gold Road south towards London. And each night, after the first, he stayed at a wayside inn or in a monastery.

On the morning of the fifth day, the pedlar and his dog came at last to the City of London. At the sight of the high walls, the pedlar's heart quickened, and so did his step.

And his mastiff leaped about, barking for excitement.

They hurried through the great gate; and there before them were crowds of people coming and going, to-ing and fro-ing; men shouting their wares; women jostling, talking; small children begging; and many, many others sitting in rags in the filthy street. And there were houses to left and right; and after that, more houses, more streets, and always more people. John had never seen such a sight nor smelt such a stink nor heard such a hubbub.

A tide of people swept him along until he came to a place where four ways met. There, John stopped a man and asked him the way to London Bridge.

'Straight on,' said the man. 'Straight as an arrow's flight, all the way.'

The broad river gleamed under the sun, silver and green, ruckled by wind; gulls swooped and climbed again, shrieking. The great bridge spanned the water, the long bridge with its houses overhanging the river. It was a sight to gladden any man. And when he saw it, John Chapman got to his knees. He thanked God that his journey had been safe, and that he had come at last to London Bridge.

But the moment the pedlar stepped on to the bridge itself he felt strangely foolish. All his hope and excitement seemed long ago. People were passing this way and that, but no one looked at John. No one took the least notice of him. Having at last found London Bridge, the poor pedlar of Swaffham felt utterly lost.

He walked up and down; he stared about him; he watched boats shoot the bridge; he added up his money. Hour after hour after hour went by; the pedlar waited.

Late that afternoon, a group of pilgrims, all with horses, gathered on the Bridge. And they began to sing: *As you came from the holy-land of Walsingham . . .*

'Walsingham!' cried John. 'I know it well. I've taken my wares there a hundred times. What does this song mean? Will *this* explain my dream?'

As if to answer him, the group of pilgrims broke up and rode off, still singing, even as he hurried towards them.

'Wait!' bawled John. 'Wait!'

But the hooves of the horses clattered and the poor pedlar was left, in the fading light, looking after them.

John felt heavy-hearted. He knew there was nothing he could do until the next morning. He wearily asked of a passer-by where he might stay, and was directed to The Three Cranes, a hostelry on the riverside, a stopping-place for passengers coming down the river, a sleeping-place for travellers in all weathers.

There John Chapman and his mastiff shared a bed of straw; they were both dog-tired.

Early on the morning of the second day the pedlar and his dog returned to the bridge. Once again, hour after hour after hour went by. John felt foolish, then lonely, then hopeless, then angry.

Late that day he saw a man with matted red hair lead on to the Bridge a loping black bear. 'Look!' he exclaimed delightedly.

And his mastiff looked, carefully.

'A rare sight!' said John. 'A sight worth travelling miles to see. Perhaps *this* is what I have travelled for. Perhaps here I shall find the meaning of my dream.' And the pedlar greeted the man; he thought he had never seen anyone so ugly in all his life. 'Does the bear dance?' he asked.

'He does,' said the man. He squinted at John. 'Give me gold and I'll show you.'

'Another time,' said the pedlar. He stooped to pat the bear's gleaming fur.

'Leave him alone!' snapped the man.

'Why?' asked John.

'He'll have your hand off, that's why.'

The pedlar stepped back hastily and called his mastiff to heel.

'He had a hand off at Cambridge,' said the man. 'So you watch it! Hands off!'

'Not the best of travelling companions,' said John.

'Mind your words,' growled the man, and he squinted more fiercely than ever. 'He'll bite your head off.'

'Like you,' said John. And with that, he walked away.

So the second day turned out no better than the first. And on the third day the poor pedlar waited and waited, he walked up and down and he walked to and fro, and no good came of it. 'Now we have only one piece of gold left,' he said to his mastiff. 'Tomorrow we'll have to go home; I'm a great fool to have come at all.'

At that moment a man shaped like an egg waddled up to John, and greeted him. 'For three days,' he said, 'you've loitered on this bridge.'

'How do you know?' asked John, surprised.

'I keep a shop here and I've seen you come and go, come and go from dawn to dusk.' He narrowed his eyes. 'What are you up to? Who are you waiting for?'

'That's exactly what I was asking myself,' said the pedlar sadly. 'To tell you the truth, I've walked to London Bridge because I dreamed that good would come of it.'

'Lord preserve me!' exclaimed the shopkeeper. 'What a waste of time!'

John Chapman shrugged his shoulders and sighed; he didn't know what to say.

'Only fools follow dreams,' said the shopkeeper. 'Why, last night I had a dream myself. I dreamed that a pot of gold lay buried by a hawthorn tree in a garden; and the garden belonged to some pedlar, in a place called Swaffham.'

32

'A pot of gold?' said John. 'A pedlar?'

'You see?' said the egg-shaped man. 'Nonsense!'

'Yes,' said John.

'Dreams are just dreams,' said the shopkeeper with a wave of his pudgy hand. 'You're wasting your time. Take my advice and go back home.'

'I will!' said John Chapman.

So it was that, in the evening of the twelfth day after his departure, John Chapman and his dog – spattered with mud, aching and blistered, weary but excited – returned home. They saw the leaning church spire; they passed the archery butts; they came at last to John's small cottage of wattle and daub.

Cateryne had never in her life been so glad to see her husband.

Margaret and Hue leaped about and their ashen hair danced on their heads. 'Come back!' cried little Dominic.

'So,' asked Cateryne, 'what of the dream, John?'

Then John told them in his own unhurried way. He told them of his journey; he told them of the long days on London Bridge; and, at last, he told them of the shopkeeper's words.

'A man follows a dream and returns with another man's dream,' said Cateryne. 'That's very strange. And how can it be true?'

'I've asked myself that a thousand times,' the pedlar said, 'and there's only one way to find out.'

The gnarled hawthorn tree stood at the end of the yard; it had lived long, perhaps hundreds of years. And now its leaves seemed to whisper secrets.

The hens clucked in the dusk; and the pig lay still, one eye open, watching John.

'I'll start here,' said the pedlar quietly. Then he gripped his round-edged spade and began to dig, firmly, rhythmically, making a mound of the loose earth.

'Can I?' asked Margaret.

'Let me!' said Hue.

'No!' said John. 'Wait!' And again he dug, firmly, rhythmically. The spade bit into the packed soil.

At once they heard it, they all heard it together, the grind of metal against metal, muted by soil. The pedlar took one look at his family and began to dig as fast as he could. Earth flew through the air. 'Look!' gasped the pedlar. 'Look! Look!' He had partly uncovered a great metal pot.

John tossed away his spade. He bent down and tugged. He worked his fingers further under the pot and tugged again. Then suddenly the dark earth gave up its secret. John staggered backwards, grasping the pot and, as he fell, the lid flew off. Coins rained on the pedlar's face; the ground was carpeted with gold.

They were all utterly silent, dumbfounded. Only the tree, the tree in the gloom went on whispering.

'John, John, what shall we do with it?' said Cateryne.

'Gather it up,' said the pedlar, slapping earth and straw from his surcoat with his great hands. 'Take it inside.'

They picked up the gold coins and put them back into the pot, and together carried it into their cottage. There they placed it on the floor, in front of the fire.

'Look! What's this?' said Hue, lifting the lid off the pot, and rubbing it. 'It's writing.'

John took the lid from him and frowned over it. 'Yes,' he said slowly, shaking his head. 'It's words.' Then John smiled. 'I know,' he said. 'I'll hide the gold here and take the empty pot with the rest of my wares to the market place. Someone is sure to come along and read it for us.'

Next morning the pedlar was early in the market place, standing over his wares with his elder children and his dog. In no time Master Fuller came picking his way towards them through the higgledy-piggledy stalls – a dark figure amongst bright colours, a silent man in a sea of noise. 'John Chapman,' he exclaimed. 'Where have you been?'

'To and fro,' said the pedlar. 'To and fro.'

'And where were you last Sunday?' asked the priest. 'I missed you at mass.'

'Well, I . . .'

'Excuses! Always excuses!' said the priest sharply. 'Who shall be saved? Men are empty vessels.' And he rapped the great metal pot with his knuckles; it rang with a fine deep note. 'Now that's a fine vessel!' said Master Fuller.

'It is,' agreed John Chapman.

'There are words on it,' said the priest. He raised the lid and narrowed his eyes.

The pedlar looked at him anxiously.

'It's in Latin,' said Master Fuller. 'It says, *Under me . . . yes . . . Under me there lies another richer than I.*' The priest frowned. 'What does that mean?' he said.

John Chapman scratched the back of his head.

'Where did you get it?'

'Out of a back yard,' said the pedlar, shrugging his broad shoulders.

'I must go,' said the priest suddenly. 'All this idle chatter. Men would do better to give time to God.' And with that, the priest walked off towards the rickety church.

At once, the pedlar packed up his wares and, led by his children, followed by his mastiff, he hurried home.

'This time you shall dig,' the pedlar told his children.

Then Hue grasped the spade and began to dig; the rounded edge sheared through the darkness. His face soon flushed; be began to pant.

'Now let Margaret have it,' the pedlar said.

Hue scowled, and handed the spade to his sister.

Then Margaret threw back her hair and stepped into the pit, and dug yet deeper. Deeper and deeper. Then, once again, metal grated against metal – the same unmistakable sound. Margaret shivered with excitement. 'You,' she said, and handed the spade back to her father.

Once more John dug as fast as he could; once more he tugged and tugged; and once more the reluctant earth yielded its secret – a second great pot, an enormous pot twice as large as the first. The pedlar could barely heave it out of the hole and on to the level ground. When he levered off the lid, they all saw that this pot too was heaped to the brim with glowing gold. 'It's like a dream,' said John, 'and because of a dream. But we're awake, and rich.'

Cateryne stared into the gaping, black hole. 'Who could have hidden it there?' she said. 'And why?'

'How shall we ever know?' replied the pedlar. 'Someone who once lived here? Travellers on the Gold Road? How can we tell? People always say the hawthorn tree is a magic tree.'

'And what are we going to do with it?' asked Cateryne.

For a moment John did not reply. His blue eyes closed, his face wrinkled. 'I know,' he said at last. 'I know. A little we'll keep – enough to pay for our own small needs, enough to buy ourselves a strip of land. But all the rest, every coin, we must give to Master Fuller to build the new church.'

Cateryne drew in her breath and smiled and clapped her hands. 'Amen!' she said.

'Amen!' chimed the children.

'In this way,' said John, 'everyone in Swaffham will share in the treasure.'

'Now,' said Cateryne, 'and in time to come.'

That afternoon, John Chapman found the priest skulking in the gloom of the tumbledown church. 'Master Fuller,' he said, 'I can give gold for the new church.'

'Every piece counts,' said the priest.

'I have many,' said John.

'Many?' said the priest suspiciously.

'Wait here,' said the pedlar. He hurried out of the church and back to his cottage. There, he counted one hundred pieces of gold for his own needs and the needs of his family, and hid them in the inner room, under the bed of straw.

Then the pedlar and his wife, and Margaret and Hue, followed by Dominic and their loyal mastiff, carried the hoard to Swaffham Church. As they crossed the market place, they shouted to their friends, 'Come with us! Come to the church!'

So the butcher, the baker, the smith, the shoemaker, and the weaver, the dyer and many another left their work. And in no time, a great procession, curious and chattering, were filing into the silent church.

In the nave, John and Cateryne turned their pot upside down.

36

Margaret and Hue did the same. A great mound of coins glowed mysteriously in the half-light.

The townspeople gasped and Master Fuller's bony face cracked into a grin; his eyes gleamed. 'Explain!' he said.

So John Chapman told them the whole story from beginning to end. And no storyteller, before or since, has ever had such an audience.

Then the priest rubbed his hands. 'There's enough gold here,' he said, 'to rebuild the north aisle, and the steeple.'

The townsfolk began to whisper excitedly.

Then the priest raised his hand, and he said, 'Let us pray, and, after that . . . let us sing and dance the night away.'

'Sing in the churchyard? Dance in the churchyard?' everyone cried.

'Even until this old church falls down,' said Master Fuller. And for the first time that anyone could remember, he laughed. He threw back his head and laughed.

So, that same evening, a man with a bugle and a man with a humstrum and a man with cymbals and clappers played as if they meaned to raise the roof off every house in Swaffham; the townsfolk sang and danced until midnight. And John the dreamer was tossed by the dancers into the air, higher and higher, towards the stars.

And his mastiff sat on his haunches, and laughed.

The Green Mist

····•━━◆━━•····

'HAVE YOU carried the light?'

'I have,' said the woman. 'Every day at sundown. I've lit it and carried it round both rooms.'

'What about the words?'

'I've spoken the words.'

'And the blood?'

'I have,' the woman said fiercely. 'Every night I've smeared it on the doorstep to scare away the horrors.'

But still the girl lay ill. One by one each neighbour called with all the same questions; pretty and ramping as she was, caring as she was, they all loved her next to their own daughters. In the back room she lay, never feeling better and slowly getting worse; no medicine cured her, no kind words cheered her for long, and people said she must be in the power of the bogles.

'She's white and waffling,' said the woman, 'like a bag of bones. And it's almost spring waking.'

The low house moaned. The wind rushed over the fen, vaulted the dykes, and keened in the village.

Day followed day and the girl grew whiter and sillier. She was no more able to stand on her own feet than a baby. She could only lie at the window, watching the winter creep away.

'It's creeping,' said the woman.

'Oh mother,' the girl kept saying over and over again, 'if only I could wake the spring with you again. If only I could wake the spring, maybe the green mist would make me strong and well, like the trees and the flowers and the young corn.'

'You'll come to the spring waking,' said the woman. 'You'll come and grow as straight and strong as ever.'

'If only,' said the girl, lying at the window.

But day after day the girl grew whiter and more wan. She looked like a snowflake melting in the sun. And day after day winter crept past; it was almost spring.

Anxiously the girl waited. But she felt so weak and so sick that she knew she would never be able to walk to the fields, and crumble bread and sprinkle salt on them with her mother and all her friends.

'I'll lift you over the doorstep,' the woman said. 'I swear I will, and you can toss out the bread with your own poor thin hands.'

'If the green mist doesn't come in the morning, I won't be able to wait. Not any longer. The soil is calling me; and the seeds swelling, the seeds bursting now will bloom over my head.'

'No,' said the woman.

'I know it,' said the girl. 'And yet, if I could see the spring wake again. . . .' Gravely she stared at the little garden that lay between the low house and the lane. 'If only I could,' she said urgently, 'I swear I'd ask no more than to live as long as one of those cowslips that grow by our gate each year.'

'Quiet!' cried the woman.

The girl looked at her, unblinking.

'Have you no sense? They're all around. You know they can hear you, the bogles.'

But the dawn of the next day brought the green mist.

The mist grew out of the ground and as the gathering light gave colour to everything, the people of the village could see that it was green.

Silently, and bringing silence with it, the mist lifted and fell and lifted, almost luminous. It swayed and reached out its long arms and wrapped itself round everything – the low fen houses and the people living in them, the trunks of trees and their topmost branches, the church spire. The green mist wove mysterious patterns over the fields and pressed itself against the side of the dyke. It was as green as grass, and fragrant as spring flowers.

The villagers got ready and met to go down to the fields, every man and woman and child who could walk; they all held bread and salt. But not the girl; she could not walk. Her mother took her from her bed and, despite her own aching bones, carried her across the room and over the doorstep, as she had promised.

The girl leaned against a door post, looking into the green mist. She looked and looked and smiled. It was everything and nothing, beckoning.

'Take this,' said the woman, standing at her side. She gave the girl bread.

The girl crumbled the bread and cast it out a little way from the doorstep.

'This,' said the woman.

The girl took the salt and cast that, too. Then she murmured the old words that were spoken each spring, the strange queer words that everyone said and no one understood.

The woman took a deep long breath and gave a grunt of satisfaction. The girl's eyes were brown, with orange irises. She smiled and, unblinking, she looked at the garden, wrapped in green. She looked at the gate where the cowslips grew.

Then her mother carried her back to her bed by the window. All morning the girl slept. Then she slept all afternoon, like a baby. Her face was unlined and untroubled. She dreamed of warm summer days and gathering flowers, the laughter of friends.

Whether or not it was the green mist, the girl began to grow stronger and prettier from that day forward. When the sun shone, she left her bed and soon left the low house. She flitted about like a will-o'-the-wisp. She danced and sang in the sunlight, as if its warmth were her life.

And the girl went visiting from house to house. All the people of the village loved her, and opened their doors wide and welcome, and felt well to see her well.

When it was cold, and late in the evenings, the girl still looked very white and wan. She crouched close to the fire, shaking. But after the spring sowing, she was able to walk with her friends along the lane, and collect flat stones, and lay bread and salt on them to get a good harvest. And when there was not one cloud in the sky for the first week in April, she and her friends trooped down to the fields with buckets; the girl spilt water in the four corners of each field and asked for rain.

By the time the cowslips had opened early in May, the girl had become strangely beautiful; her friends looked at her and thought they could almost see through her; she laughed often enough, but often she was so silent, and they wondered what she was thinking. They all knew each other like brother and sister, living as they did a few yards apart in the middle of the great empty marsh; but now they felt that they did not quite know her, and were almost afraid of her.

Every morning the girl knelt by the cowslips at the garden gate. She watered them and tended them, and danced beside them in the sunlight.

'Leave them alone!' the woman called.

The girl took no notice.

'Let them be,' ordered the woman, coming out of the low house, abrupt and anxious. 'Leave them alone, or I'll pull them up.'

Then the girl stopped dancing and looked at the woman strangely. 'Mother,' she said in a soft low voice, 'don't even pick one of those flowers unless you're tired of me.'

The woman pressed her lips together.

'They'll fade soon enough; soon enough, yes, as you know.'

Early one evening a boy from the village stopped by the gate to gossip with the girl and the woman. The sun cast long shadows and a light, slight wind breathed around them: just the time for passing time!

The boy picked a flower and twirled it between his fingers as they talked – talked of the birth of a baby, and a midsummer marriage; talked of the fen that was full of prying bogles and horrible boggarts; talked of the need to improve the dyke, with no thought or knowledge of the world and its worries beyond.

Out across the marsh the wind started forward. It sprang over the dyke, tousled and interrupted them.

'That's it, then,' said the boy, standing off.

The woman smiled and nodded.

The girl suddenly tightened and trembled. 'You,' she said, staring at the boy's feet. 'Did you pull that cowslip?' She looked strange and white, and pressed her right hand over her heart.

The boy glanced down; then he stooped and scooped it up. He looked at the girl, thinking he had never really noticed quite how lovely and different she was. 'Here you are,' he said, offering her the flower, grinning.

The girl took the cowslip. She stared at the flower, and at the boy, and everything about her; at the green trees, and the sprouting grass, and the yellow blooms, and up at the golden shining sun. Then, all at once, shrinking as if the sunlight that she loved so much were burning her, the girl turned and ran into the low house. She said nothing; she only gave a sort of cry, like a poor dumb beast in pain. And she caught the cowslip close against her heart.

The girl lay huddled on her bed. She did not move. She did not move at all. She stared at the flower in her hand as it faded, hour by hour.

'Come,' said the woman, and offered her food, drink, and friendly talk.

But the girl said nothing, and night came on. She never spoke again.

At dawn, lying on the bed, there was only a white dead shrunken thing, with a shrivelled cowslip in its hand. The woman covered it with a quilt, and thought of the beautiful laughing girl, dancing like a bird in the sunshine, down by the yellow nodding flowers. Only yesterday, she thought. 'Yesterday,' she whispered to herself.

The bogles had heard her and given the girl her wish. She had bloomed with the cowslips and faded with the first of them.

'It's all true,' the woman whispered, 'true as death.'

The Callow Pit Coffer

'KEEP AWAY from Callow Pit,' said Thor, the old cottar, and he stabbed at the fire with his stick.

Thor's three sons, Jakke, and Keto and the little cripple Simpkin had heard his warning before. 'That place, it's haunted. It's unnatural.' He had told them a hundred times if he had told them once.

And Simpkin shivered.

But Jakke and Keto glanced at one another; their eyes shifted with some deep secret only they shared.

Jakke was the elder brother, ill at ease with other men, a skinflint with words. Yet he loved animals of every kind, and hated to see them suffer the slings of winter; and he was always gentle with Simpkin.

Keto was the rogue everyone liked, the practical-joker, the poacher who pinched Sir Jocelin's rabbits and hares and, best of all, his fleet deer; he was red-haired as a fox.

But Jakke and Keto had things in common too: they were both big men, fine wrestlers; they were both brave; danger excited them.

Danger: that was Thor's warning. 'There are spirits and phantoms at Callow Pit,' he said. 'And that's where the headless horseman rides.' He jabbed again at the fire. 'If you have to pass it, keep your mouths shut. Remember the saying, *if you don't bother them with words, they won't bother you.*'

Callow Pit lay under the shadow of a bald hill, in a gloomy hollow where four ways met. One day the water rose high, the next it sank mysteriously low.

The stories about it, even the sight of it terrified Thor and almost all the other people of Southwood. If you peered into the water, it was so dark you could not see your own face.

'Face to face to face to face, you only give, I only take,' warbled the simpleton Odda. But no one listened to him, neither Thor and his sons, nor anyone else; perhaps he was wiser than they knew.

'I *saw* the headless horseman,' whispered Edmund the young cottar, to his new wife Emma, new to him, new to the hamlet. 'I saw him as he galloped up from the Spon. He rides past Southwood church, skirting the graveyard, on and on, and disappears near Callow Pit.'

'You're shivering, Edmund,' said Emma, and wound her arms about him.

Everyone knew Callow Pit was evil. Its black eye watched the world, unblinking. The two oak trees beside it had been struck by lightning, and withered and died.

But everyone in Southwood knew another thing.

'Gold,' said Thor, 'at the bottom of the pit.' He leaned forward on his stick, nodding his grizzled head, and confided, 'In an iron coffer, gold and silver.'

'Like the sun and the moon,' sighed Simpkin.

'Like your hair,' whispered Edmund to Emma, in their hut.

'How did it get there?' said Emma.

'Some people say Danes left it there and never lived to collect it; others that King Edmund concealed it there in case the Danes should get it; and some are sure our grandfather's fathers hid it when Duke William came. Where did it come from? Nobody knows.' Edmund paused. 'But God knows, we could do with it now, with that devil Sir Jocelin for lord, and the worst of winter still to come.'

'Go, then,' said Emma. With her blue eyes, she teased him. 'If you love me, go and get it.'

Edmund stared at her, speechless; a shiver rippled down his spine.

Then Emma burst into laughter, and Edmund laughed too. But he felt disquieted all the same, and wished she had not suggested such a thing, even in jest.

Then they prayed together: 'Save us from starving and freezing, O God; O God, give us our daily bread.'

And Odda, the simpleton, in his hut, said to himself, 'Brr! Poor Odda's heart is gold, but the devil's in him.'

Then the north wind blew over the hill and through the hamlet. The freezing blasts carried off everyone's words.

But the very same idea that disquieted Edmund was already at work in the minds of Jakke and Keto. For that was their secret. They were planning to go to Callow Pit by night, and there to fish for gold. If Thor had known their intention, he would have tried to stop them, and sworn by St William of Norwich that no good could come of it.

'This story, that story about Callow Pit!' said Jakke contemptuously. 'I don't believe in them. Old men's chatter! Old wives' tales!' His eyes were the colour of iron. 'If there's gold, I must get it. Think! Think of all we could do with it! We could walk to Norwich fair, buy horses there, ride home laden with salted meat and corn . . .'

'If you go, I go,' interrupted Keto. His scalp tingled at the idea, for he half believed in the stories himself. But the danger only made him all the more eager. 'There'd be enough,' he exclaimed, 'enough for us, for father and Simpkin, enough for everyone in Southwood.'

'All right,' agreed Jakke. 'The two of us!'

'When shall we go?' asked Keto.

'As soon as possible,' Jakke replied. 'Tonight, when nobody's about.'

And so they put their heads together and laid their plans, down to the smallest detail.

As soon as they were sure that Thor and Simpkin were asleep, Jakke and Keto crept out of the smoky hut. Icy fingers of air burned through their clothing.

'Listen!' whispered Jakke.

In his own hut, Odda was singing softly: 'Beware, I'm an eye, I see you coming. I'll be silent, I'll say nothing. Please say nothing, heal me, heal me, heal me.' And his voice was pure as the single bird which defied the darkness and the cold, and cheeped from its perch in the alder tree.

Jakke cocked his head to one side, listening.

'Come on,' Keto whispered urgently. 'We haven't got all night.'

'We have,' said Jakke.

Then the brothers stole away from Southwood under the stars

47

and the bruised moon. They hurried past the hut where Edmund and Emma lay asleep, strode across the common land and round the two open fields, towards the manor of Sir Jocelin de Neville. With them they brought a long leather thong, and an oak staff with an iron hook. Now they needed Sir Jocelin's ladders.

The manor walls were darker than the darkness. Jakke and Keto stepped through the great gateway and across the deserted courtyard. Their boots crunched on the gravel.

Jakke gritted his teeth. 'Quick!'

'There!' said Keto.

They sprang across the yard and snatched up the ladders from beneath the hay loft.

'Come on!' urged Jakke.

At once he and Keto hoisted the ladders between them, one on either shoulder.

But Sir Jocelin's wolfhounds, tethered in their kennels, had heard them. They opened their fanged jaws and barked ferociously.

The two brothers, carrying the ladders between them, loped awkwardly across the yard and under the gateway arch once more.

The sound of the barking receded; darkness received them.

'Goodness!' gasped Keto. 'Better the devil himself than Sir Jocelin's wolfhounds.'

Then, after regaining their breath, they set off once more and, falling into step, strode towards the crossways, and Callow Pit.

'Well!' said Jakke as they approached the pit. 'Are you ready?'

Keto nodded.

'Good,' said Jakke. 'And remember . . .'

'What was that?' said Keto stiffening. The nape of his neck tingled.

Jakke stood motionless. 'What?' he said. 'I didn't hear anything.'

'Hooves,' said Keto. 'The drumming of hooves.'

'I heard nothing,' said Jakke.

A small buffeting wind had got up, a night wind from nowhere, and with it a few clouds that scudded before the moon. It was darker than it was before.

'I said we hadn't got all night,' whispered Keto.

Jakke scowled, and put two fingers to his lips. 'Remember,' he said in a low voice. 'Quiet now.'

So they came to the hollow where four ways met. The first way led to Southwood, the second to the sea, the third lost itself in a thicket, and the fourth plunged through a cutting where demons lived.

The bald back of the hill sheltered Callow Pit. The water was still. It was black. It looked like pitch. The grey torsos of the blasted oaks leaned over it.

Jakke and Keto stared down at the pool, then stared at each other. Now they were filled with doubts, and all the stories about Callow Pit crowded into their minds. . . .

Then Jakke moved forward, and Keto followed him. He had to, for he was carrying the other end of the ladders! They kneeled at the pit's edge and, putting the ladders end to end, bound them tightly together with a leather thong.

Then Jakke motioned to Keto to hold one end and, grasping the other, stepped cautiously round the pool. At last, he stood opposite. Each lowered his end on to the damp soil; they had bridged Callow Pit.

Now Keto, carrying the staff, joined Jakke on the other side. The two brothers peered into the pool; there was no going back now. Keto handed the staff to Jakke, and at once Jakke stepped out, a rung at a time, over Callow Pit. One rung, two rungs, three rungs, four rungs. Five rungs – the bank already looked a long way off. Keto, like a henchman, followed two rungs behind him. The ladders held firm. They were stout, and strongly bound.

Now Jakke grasped the staff more firmly; his knuckles gleamed like ivory. Then he drew in his breath and plunged the hook into the water.

A raven screeched, starting from its hideout in the oak stump. Jakke leaned forward and prodded the bottom of the pit. And Keto watched, anxiously.

Jakke straightened, shook his head, drew the dripping staff out of the water and awkwardly turned about. Then he plunged it in a second time.

The result was just the same.

So the two brothers stepped forward again until Keto stood in the very middle of the pit. His blood whirled; he felt giddy. He took the staff from Jakke and rammed it into the water.

Be calm, Keto, be careful, Jakke gestured with his hands.

Now Keto sank the iron-hooked staff into the water again.

'Cluung!' They heard it directly; the clang of metal against metal underneath the water.

Keto drew in his breath sharply. He went down on one knee and probed more carefully. It *feels* like the coffer, he thought. It's the right shape. It *is* the coffer!

Suddenly, the iron hook was snagged. Keto pulled at the staff; some force had caught against it. He pulled harder, and harder, and the weight began to move.

Then Jakke crouched forward and gripped the staff as well. He tugged with all his strength. The ladders groaned. And slowly, slowly, swaying like drunkards, the two brothers lifted up and out of the water, inch by inch, a dripping, crusted, iron coffer.

They gasped at it: at its weight; at the great lock on it; at the massive ring in its lid which had snagged their hook.

Carefully, they lowered it on to the ladders, and the ladders creaked and complained more angrily, and sagged at the centre.

Oh the gold and the silver, thought Keto. His mind sang like a bird. Food for us, for Thor and Simpkin, for everyone else . . . this winter, every winter . . . not one piece for Sir Jocelin. . . .

Jakke tapped Keto on the shoulder and took the staff from him. He slipped it through the ring so that they could sling the coffer between them. Then each brother put one end of the staff over his shoulder. The gold seemed light as a load of feathers. They were rich, more than rich; they were ready to go.

Keto was so elated he could have climbed to the moon. The stars in the sky seemed to spray like sparks over him. He tossed his head and shouted gaily: 'We've got it, we've got it; the devil himself can't get it from us now.'

Then at once a yellowish mist surged up from the water, and swirled angrily about them. It caught at their throats; they coughed and spluttered and choked.

Birds shrieked out of the stillness of night; the air was full of the flapping of wings. Wolves howled. Grass blades stiffened. The hackles of all natural things rose at the unnatural.

'Quick!' yelled Jakke. 'Quick, Keto!'

It was too late. Out of the water thrust a hideous black hand, then a huge black arm.

Jakke and Keto curdled with terror and recoiled. A step further, and they would have toppled backwards into the pit.

The unearthly hand clawed at the ladder; its nails were like spikes. Keto bared his teeth. 'Don't let go,' he growled, terrified, yet furiously determined not to lose the coffer.

Jakke responded. He crushed his end of the staff in his grip. Face to face with the powers of darkness, Jakke and Keto found strength in themselves; they pulled like demons. The ladders groaned and curved like a crossbow; cold water gripped their ankles.

Then the arm wound round the coffer, and yanked it. Jakke and Keto lurched forward on their toes, rocked back on to their heels. They refused to let go.

'Pull, pull,' urged Keto. 'PULL!'

The yellow vapour wrapped them in its hundred arms; the oak staff stood firm, stronger than them all.

The brothers pulled again, with the strength of ten men. Then metal screamed; the coffer and the ring in its lid were torn apart.

Jakke and Keto cried out as they fell backwards into the water; and the coffer, the coffer hit the surface of the pool with a colossal splash. It disappeared from sight.

Sodden and shivering, still in possession of the staff and ring, Jakke and Keto sat on the damp earth, a little way off from the pit.

For what seemed like a long time, neither of them spoke. Fowls returned to their perches; wolves no longer howled. Already, the cold green light of dawn showed in the east.

At last, Jakke broke the silence. All he said was, 'Keto, Keto.'

And Keto shook his head dumbly.

So the coffer they had not, because Keto had forgotten the saying, and spoken the words; but they had the ring for their pains – the massive iron ring as a proof of their exploit.

Jakke and Keto looked at it and fingered it, wonderingly.

Yellow tinged the pale green of the east; all was not lost even if the coffer was lost.

Jake stood up and stretched. 'We should go now,' he said.

'The ladders,' said Keto in a small voice. His arms ached so much that he didn't know how he would be able to carry them back to the manor.

'Confound the ladders!' said Jakke.

So the two brothers took the way to Southwood; and presently the lead melted out of their feet, and they swung their arms. They began to talk about what had happened, and especially about the black hand; the thought of it, huge and hideous in their minds, was worse even than the sight of it.

Keto cursed his wagging tongue that had cost them the gold. 'I'm sorry, Jakke,' he said, simply and humbly.

Jakke turned to him. 'If you don't bother them . . .' he said. And he was scowling and grinning at one and the same time.

'Where have you been?' demanded Thor angrily as soon as Jakke and Keto stepped into the hut. He saw they were haggard and soaked to the skin. He glared at them under his thunderous brows. 'Where have you been? What's that ring?'

'We'll tell you,' said Keto.

'You will,' said Thor. 'I'm still your father, aren't I. Where have you been?'

'Callow Pit,' said Jakke.

'Where?' exploded Thor.

'Callow Pit,' repeated Jakke, as if he had just been round to Edmund's hut.

And Simpkin, sitting in the corner, flaxen-haired, stared up at his brothers as if they were ghosts.

'You see this ring?' said Keto, lifting it between his hands like a crown.

'What is it?' muttered Thor uneasily.

So, sodden and exhausted as they were, Jakke and Keto told them the whole story, from first to last. And Thor, who had begun by being angry and fearful, ended by being fearful and proud.

Simpkin, too, glowed with pride at the daring of his brothers. But there was an ache in heart because he had not gone with them, because he had never shared their adventures and never would. It was not envy now, though once it had been so; it was simply a sadness to be endured.

Then Thor hurried out into the sharp, early morning air. Thin streams of smoke rose from each hut. He was full of the story, anxious to tell anyone and everyone, and as quickly as he could.

He was not disappointed. In all his life, he had never been paid so much attention. In the two fields that day, and over food, and in the smoky firelight, Jakke and Keto and Callow Pit were the only topic of conversation.

Edmund and Emma listened to the story standing shoulder to shoulder; and as it unfolded, their eyes opened wider and wider. Then Edmund remembered how Emma had dared him to go to Callow Pit; he felt uneasy once more, and almost a coward, and envied Jakke and Keto even as he praised them for their great bravery.

But Emma, she trembled at the thought of how Edmund might have taken her seriously, and gone to Callow Pit. And now she wished as Edmund had wished before, that she had not suggested such a thing at all, even in fun.

But then their eyes met; and, as always, they soon forgot everything, even the story, except one another.

When the tale was told in the hearing of Odda, he sat bolt upright and listened most attentively: and later he was heard to say sagely, sadly: 'I am what I was, alas, alas. Dark's still in me; dispossess me.'

'What shall we do with the ring?' said Keto.

'I'm not having it in here,' said Thor at once. 'It's an evil thing. Throw it away.'

'Evil?' said Jakke. 'Why should it be evil?'

'In any case, continued Keto, 'it's a proof and a reminder.'

'It's a warning,' Thor growled.

So they sat in silence for a long time, because they did not know what to do with the ring.

'I know,' said Simpkin. 'I know, you could fix it to the church door. People will see it there, now and always. . . .'

Jakke and Keto nodded approvingly.

'And if *you* are right,' Simpkin continued, turning to his father, 'then its evil will be useless on sacred ground. You can commend it to the mercy of the saints.'

Simpkin's suggestion pleased them all. And so, in due course, after Thor had explained their purpose to the priest, the massive ring was secured to the door of St Edmund's Church.

Anyone could go to see it there, and everyone did. Pedlars and pilgrims, travelling quacks and tinkers and other passers-by came to visit the church at Southwood.

Then they visited the tavern; the traffic there in mead and ale was immense. And it put gold into the pockets of the people of Southwood, perhaps even as much as was in the coffer.

After Jakke and Keto had told their story, no one went too close to Callow Pit again, or had the least desire to risk their lives for gold. Those who had to pass it, walking or riding along the four ways, screwed up their eyes and turned their heads in the opposite direction.

And though years passed, the fear remained. It still remains, just as the coffer still lies in the dark fist of Callow Pit.

Lightning has struck other oaks nearby; in summer and in winter the hill brow broods; at times some people hear the distant thunder of hooves; and now, as always, the trumpet of wind blasts from the north.

The Dauntless Girl

'DANG IT!' said the farmer.

'Why?' said the miller.

'Not a drop left,' the farmer said.

'Not one?' asked the blacksmith, raising his glass and inspecting it. His last inch of whisky glowed like molten honey in the flickering firelight.

'Why not?' said the miller.

'You fool!' said the farmer. 'Because the bottle's empty.' He peered into the flames. 'Never mind that though,' he said. 'We'll send out my Mary. She'll go down to the inn and bring us another bottle.'

'What?' said the blacksmith. 'She'll be afraid to go out on such a dark night, all the way down to the village, and all on her own.'

'Never!' said the farmer. 'She's afraid of nothing – nothing live or dead. She's worth all my lads put together.'

The farmer gave a shout and Mary came out of the kitchen. She stood and she listened. She went out into the dark night and in a little time she returned with another bottle of whisky.

The miller and the blacksmith were delighted. They drank to her health, but later the miller said, 'That's a strange thing, though.'

'What's that?' asked the farmer.

'That she should be so bold, your Mary.'

'Bold as brass,' said the blacksmith. 'Out and alone and the night so dark.'

'That's nothing at all,' said the farmer. 'She'd go anywhere, day or night. She's afraid of nothing – nothing live or dead.'

'Words,' said the blacksmith. 'But my, this whisky tastes good.'

'Words nothing,' said the farmer. 'I bet you a golden guinea that neither of you can name anything that girl will not do.'

The miller scratched his head and the blacksmith peered at the golden guinea of whisky in his glass. 'All right,' said the blacksmith. 'Let's meet here again at the same time next week. Then I'll name something Mary will not do.'

Next week the blacksmith went to see the priest and borrowed the key of the church door from him. Then he paid a visit to the sexton and showed him the key.

'What do you want with that?' asked the sexton.

'What I want with you,' said the blacksmith, 'is this. I want you to go into the church tonight, just before midnight, and hide yourself in the dead house.'

'Never,' said the sexton.

'Not for half a guinea?' asked the blacksmith.

The old sexton's eyes popped out of his head. 'Dang it!' he said. 'What's that for then?'

'To frighten that brazen farm girl, Mary,' said the blacksmith, grinning. 'When she comes to the dead house, just give a moan or a holler.'

The old sexton's desire for the half guinea was even greater than his fear. He hummed and hawed and at last he agreed to do as the blacksmith asked.

Then the blacksmith clumped the sexton on the back with his massive fist and the old sexton coughed. 'I'll see you tomorrow,' said the blacksmith, 'and settle the account. Just before midnight, then! Not a minute later!'

The sexton nodded and the blacksmith strode up to the farm. Darkness was falling and the farmer and the miller were already drinking and waiting for him.

'Well?' said the farmer.

The blacksmith grasped his glass then raised it and rolled the whisky around his mouth.

'Well,' said the farmer. 'Are you or aren't you?'

'This,' said the blacksmith, 'is what your Mary will not do. She won't go into the church alone at midnight. . . .'

'No,' said the miller.

'. . . and go to the dead house,' continued the blacksmith, 'and bring back a skull bone. That's what she won't do.'

'Never,' said the miller.

The farmer gave a shout and Mary came out of the kitchen. She stood and she listened; and later, at midnight, she went out into the darkness and walked down to the church.

Mary opened the church door. She held up her lamp and clattered down the steps to the dead house. She pushed open its creaking door and saw skulls and thigh bones and bones of every kind gleaming in front of her. She stooped and picked up the nearest skull bone.

'Let that be,' moaned a muffled voice from behind the dead house door. 'That's my mother's skull bone.'

So Mary put that skull down and picked up another.

'Let that be,' moaned a muffled voice from behind the dead house door. 'That's my father's skull bone.'

So Mary put that skull bone down too and picked up yet another one. And, as she did so, she angrily called out, 'Father or mother, sister or brother, I *must* have a skull bone and that's my last word.' Then she walked out of the dead house, slammed the door, and hurried up the steps and back up to the farm.

Mary put the skull bone on the table in front of the farmer. 'There's your skull bone, master,' she said, and started off for the kitchen.

'Wait a minute!' said the farmer, grinning and shivering at one and the same time. 'Didn't you hear anything in the dead house, Mary?'

'Yes,' she said. 'Some fool of a ghost called out to me: 'Let that be! That's my mother's skull bone' and 'Let that be! That's my father's skull bone.' But I told him straight: 'Father or mother, sister or brother, I *must* have a skull bone.'

The miller and the blacksmith stared at Mary and shook their heads.

'So I took one,' said Mary, 'and here I am and here it is.' She looked down at the three faces flickering in the firelight. 'As I was going away,' she said, 'after I had locked the door, I heard the old ghost hollering and shrieking like mad.'

The blacksmith and the miller looked at each other and got to their feet.

'That'll do then, Mary,' said the farmer.

The blacksmith knew that the sexton must have been scared out of his wits at being locked all alone in the dead house. They all raced down to the church, and clattered down the steps into the dead house, but they were too late. They found the old sexton lying stone dead on his face.

'That's what comes to trying to frighten a poor young girl,' said the farmer.

So the blacksmith gave the farmer a golden guinea and the farmer gave it to his Mary.

Mary and her daring were known in every house. And after her visit to the dead house, and the death of the old sexton, her fame spread for miles and miles around.

One day the squire, who lived three villages off, rode up to the farm and asked the farmer if he could talk to Mary.

'I've heard,' said the squire, 'that you're afraid of nothing.'

Mary nodded.

'Nothing live or dead,' said the farmer proudly.

'Listen then!' said the squire. 'Last year my old mother died and was buried. But she will not rest. She keeps coming back into the house, and especially at mealtimes.'

Mary stood and listened.

'Sometimes you can see her, sometimes you can't. And when you can't, you can still see a knife and fork get up off the table and play about where her hands would be.'

'That's a strange thing altogether,' said the farmer, 'that she should go on walking.'

'Strange and unnatural,' said the squire. 'And now my servants won't stay with me, not one of them. They're all afraid of her.'

The farmer sighed and shook his head. 'Hard to come by, good servants,' he said.

'So,' said the squire, 'seeing as she's afraid of nothing, nothing live or dead, I'd like to ask your girl to come and work with me.'

Mary was pleased at the prospect of such good employment and, sorry as he was to lose her, the farmer saw there was nothing for it but to let her go.

'I'll come,' said the girl. 'I'm not afraid of ghosts. But you ought to take account of that in my wages.'

'I will,' said the squire.

So Mary went back with the squire to be his servant. The first thing she always did was to lay a place for the ghost at table, and she took great care not to let the knife and fork lie criss-cross.

At meals, Mary passed the ghost the meat and vegetables and sauce and gravy. And then she said: 'Pepper, madam?' and 'Salt, madam?'

The ghost of the squire's mother was pleased enough. Things went on the same from day to day until the squire had to go up to London to settle some legal business.

Next morning Mary was down on her knees, cleaning the parlour grate, when she noticed something thin and glimmering push in through the parlour door, which was just ajar; when it got inside the room, the shape began to swell and open out. It was the old ghost.

For the first time, the ghost spoke to the girl. 'Mary,' she said in a hollow voice, 'are you afraid of me?'

'No, madam,' said Mary. 'I've no cause to be afraid of you, for you are dead and I'm alive.'

For a while the ghost looked at the girl kneeling by the parlour grate. 'Mary,' she said, 'will you come down into the cellar with me? You mustn't bring a light – but I'll shine enough to light the way for you.'

So the two of them went down the cellar steps and the ghost shone like an old lantern. When they got down to the bottom, they went down a passage, and took a right turn and a left, and then the ghost pointed to some loose tiles in one corner. 'Pick up those tiles,' she said.

Mary did as she was asked. And underneath the tiles were two bags of gold, a big one and a little one.

The ghost quivered. 'Mary,' she said, 'that big bag is for your master. But that little bag is for you, for you are a dauntless girl and deserve it.'

Before Mary could open the bag or even open her mouth, the old ghost drifted up the steps and out of sight. She was never seen again and Mary had a devil of a time groping her way along the dark passage and up out of the cellar.

After three days, the squire came back from London.

'Good morning, Mary,' he said. 'Have you seen anything of my mother while I've been away?'

'Yes, sir,' said Mary. 'That I have.' She opened her eyes wide. 'And if you aren't afraid of coming down into the cellar with me, I'll show you something.'

The squire laughed. 'I'm not afraid if you're not afraid,' he said, for the dauntless girl was a very pretty girl.

So Mary lit a candle and led the squire down into the cellar, walked down the passage, took a right turn and a left, and raised the loose tiles in the corner for a second time.

'Two bags,' said the squire.

'Two bags of gold,' said Mary. 'The little one is for you and the big one is for me.'

'Lor! said the squire, and he said nothing else. He did think that his mother might have given him the big bag, as indeed she had, but all the same he took what he could.

After that, Mary always crossed the knives and forks at mealtimes to prevent the old ghost from telling what she had done.

The squire thought things over: the gold and the ghost and Mary's good looks. What with one thing and another he proposed to Mary, and the dauntless girl, she accepted him. In a little while they married, and so the squire did get both bags of gold after all.

Tiddy Mun

BEFORE THE DYKES were dug, there was marsh and more marsh, as far as the eye could see.

The whole place teemed with boggarts and will-o'-the-wykes and other evil creatures. In the darkness, hands without arms reached out of the water and beckoned; voices of the dead cried and moaned all night long; and goblins danced on the tussocks. There were witches too; they mounted the great black snags of peat, and turned them into snakes and raced about on them in the water. No wonder people stayed indoors after nightfall. The marsh was no place to be after dark, and when some man did have to make his way home along the marsh-paths by lamplight, he shook with fright – his skin crawled with terror from the crown of his head to the tips of his toes.

But there was another spirit living in the marshes. He had no name and everyone called him Tiddy Mun.

Tiddy Mun lived in the deep and dark green water-holes that never moved from dawn to dusk. But when the evening mist dipped and lifted and dipped over the marsh, Tiddy Mun rose to the surface and hoisted himself on to some marsh path. He went creeping through the darkness, limpelty lobelty, like a dear little old grand-father with long white hair and a long white beard, all matted and tangled; he hobbled along, limpelty lobelty, wearing a grey gown so that people could scarcely make him out from the mist. His move-ment was the sound of running water and the sough of the wind, and his laugh was like the screech of a peewit.

No one was scared of Tiddy Mun like they were of the boggarts. He wasn't wicked and chancy like the water-wraiths; and he wasn't white and creepy like the dead hands. All the same, it was kind of scary to sit in front of your own fire and then hear a screeching laugh right outside the door, a screeching laugh passing by in a skirl of wind and water.

Tiddy Mun did no one any harm and there were times when he did people a really good turn. When rain fell day after day, and the water level rose in the marshes and crept up to the doors, and soaked the bundles of straw strewn over people's floors, a whole family – father and mother and children – would go out into the darkness or the night of the new moon. They stared out over the marshes and called out together, 'Tiddy Mun, without a name, Tiddy Mun, the waters are washing through.'

The children clung to their mother, and their mother clung to her husband, and they all stood shaking and shivering in the darkness. Then they heard the peewit-screech over the swamp. That was Tiddy Mun's reply. Sure enough, in the morning the water level had dropped and the bundles of straw were dry again. And that was Tiddy Mun's doing.

Then outsiders moved in, rich farmers and surveyors and, after them, gangs of Dutchmen. They said it was high time the marshes were drained, and told fine stories about how the mist would lift once and for all, and how the swamps would be turned into fields, and how no one would suffer from marsh-fever ever again.

The marshmen were against that. They knew the cause of their aches and complaints, and that when they were not shaking with fear because of the boggarts, as often as not they were shaking with the fevers and agues that rose from the marshes. But they were used to them and used to the look of the place; it was their home. 'Bad is bad,' they said, 'but meddling is worse.'

Above all, the marshmen took against the Dutchmen who had come over the sea to dig and drain around them. They wouldn't give them food, or bedding, or even greet them in passing. Everyone muttered that it would be an ill day for them all when the marshes were drained and Tiddy Mun was angered.

All the same, the marshmen were unable to do anything about it. The Dutchmen dug and drew the water off; they emptied the water-holes so that they were as dry as two-year-old Mothering Cakes. The dykes got longer and longer, and deeper and deeper; the water ran away, and ran away down to the river, and the whole soppy, quivering swamp was turned into firm land. The marshmen saw that the soft black bog would soon be replaced by green fields.

Then, one day, one of the Dutchmen disappeared. And, soon afterwards, a second one followed him. They were spirited away! The work gangs searched for them and searched for them, but not a shadow of them was ever seen again. The marshmen nodded; they knew well enough that they would never find them, not if they searched until the golden Beasts of Judgement came roaring and ramping over the land to fetch away sinners.

The old marshmen wagged their heads and their children wagged their tongues and said, 'That's what comes of crossing Tiddy Mun!'

But the outsiders, the rich farmers and surveyors, were not to be put off. They brought in one work gang after another and although Tiddy Mun drowned many of them, the work of draining the marshes slowly progressed. The marshmen were helpless and, soon enough, there were worse disasters.

The marshmen's own cows began to pine, their pigs starved and their ponies went lame. The children fell sick, lambs died, and new milk curdled. Thatched roofs fell in, walls burst at the seams, and everything was arsy-versy.

At first the marshmen couldn't think who or what had caused such trouble. They said it was the work of the witches or the goblins. They turned on Sally, the old woman with the evil eye who could charm dead men out of their graves, and ducked her in the horse-pond until she was more dead than alive; they all said the Lord's Prayer backwards; and they spat to the east to keep the goblins away. But it was no good. Tiddy Mun himself was angry and upset with them all.

What could they do? Little children sickened in their mothers' arms; all the poor white faces never brightened but became more and more wan. Their fathers sat and puffed their pipes and their mothers cried over their little innocent babies, lying so white and smiling and peaceful. Tiddy Mun's anger was like a frost that comes and kills the prettiest flowers.

The marshmen's hearts were heavy and their stomachs were empty, what with the sickness and the bad harvest and this, that and the other. They knew something must be done, and done soon, before it was too late and they were all dead and gone.

Then one man thought of the old times. 'Remember before the delving?' he said. 'Remember how, when the waters rose, we went out into the night under the new moon, and called out to Tiddy Mun?'

'He heard us then,' said another man, 'and he did as we asked him.'

'Let's call on him again,' said the first man.

The marshmen talked. They thought that if they called out to Tiddy Mun, to show that they wished him well and would give him back the water if only they could, he might lift the curse on them all and forgive them again.

Before darkness fell on the night of the next new moon, there was a great gathering of marshfolk down by the largest of the dykes across the marsh. They came in threes and fours, jumping at every sough of the wind and starting at every snag of stranded peat. They need not have worried. The poor old boggarts and will-o'-the-wykes had been entirely dug out, all the swamp-bogles had followed the waters and flitted away.

While it slowly grew dark, they all huddled together. They whispered and watched, and kept an eye on the shadows over their shoulders; they listened uneasily to the skirling of the wind and the lip-lap of the running water. And every single one of them – man, woman and child – carried a stoup of fresh water in his hands.

At long last it was night. They all stood on the edge of the dyke, and loudly they all called out together, as if with one voice: 'Tiddy Mun, without a name, here's water for you, water for you, lift your curse.'

Then they tipped the water out of their stoups and into the dyke – splash sploppert!

The marshmen listened, a small scared huddle clinging to one another in the middle of the stillness. They listened to see if Tiddy Mun would answer them; but there was nothing but a great unnatural stillness.

And then, just when they thought it was all in vain, the most terrible whimpering and wailing broke out all around them. It surged to and fro and sounded for all the world like a crowd of little babies crying their hearts out, with no one to comfort them. They sobbed and sobbed themselves almost into silence; and then they began again, louder than ever, wailing and moaning until it made the heart ache to hear them.

Suddenly, one mother after another began to cry out that it was her dead baby, calling on Tiddy Mun to lift the curse, and to let the marsh children live and grow strong.

Then, out of the dark air overhead, the babies moaned and gently whimpered, as if they recognised their mothers' voices and were trying to find their breasts.

'A little hand touched me,' one woman said.

'Cold lips kissed me,' said another woman.

They all said they felt soft wings fluttering round them as they stood and listened to that mournful greeting.

Then, all at once, there was complete stillness again. The marshmen could hear the water lapping at their feet, and a dog yelping in a distant hut.

And then, out of the river itself, soft and fond came the old peewit-screech. Once and a second time: it was Tiddy Mun.

And the marshmen, they all knew he would lift his curse. How they laughed and shouted and ran and jumped, like a pack of children coming out of school, as they set off home with light hearts and never a thought of the boggarts.

But the marsh women followed slowly. They were all silent, thinking of their babies. Their arms felt empty and their hearts lonely and weary because of the cold kiss, the fluttering of the little fingers. They wept as they thought of their little babies, drifting to and fro in the moaning of the night wind.

From that day, things began to change and prosper. Sick children got well, cattle chewed the cud and the bacon-pigs fattened. The marshmen earned good money and there was bread in plenty. Tiddy Mun had indeed lifted his curse.

But every new moon, all the marsh folk – men and women and children – went into the darkness and down to the edge of the dyke. There they tipped their stoups into the dyke and cried out, 'Tiddy Mun, without a name, here's water for you, water for you.'

Then out of the river itself, soft and tender and pleased rose the peewit-screech. And the marshmen went back to their houses, happy and contented.

But one thing is certain. If any man failed to go down to the dyke without good reason, unless he were ill, Tiddy Mun missed him and was angry with him, and laid the curse upon him worse than ever. There was nothing he could do about it until the next new moon, when he went down to the dyke with the others to beg that the curse should be lifted. And when children misbehaved, their parents warned them that Tiddy Mun would spirit them away; they were as good as gold after that, for they all knew the warnings were true enough.

Every marshman knew that little figure, limping by in the mist, all grey and white, screeching like a peewit. But one month, when the marshmen trooped down to the dyke at new moon, and called out to Tiddy Mun, they got no reply. It was the same the next month, and the month after. Without warning, Tiddy Mun had vanished.

Why did he go? Perhaps he was frightened away by all the changes and new machines in Lincolnshire. And where did he go? Perhaps he is here, perhaps he is there, Tiddy Mun. Only listen for the laugh in a skirl of wind and the sound of running water.

The Black Dog of Bungay

'THAT'S A queer old morning,' said the man.

'That's been a queer summer,' his wife replied.

True, it hadn't rained on St Swithin's Day. And true, the hay harvest was laid in, no worse than most years and better than some. But as everyone agreed, it was impossible to say what the weather would be like from one day to the next.

'Hear that?' said the man.

His wife stopped and listened.

'Hear it?' said the man. 'The redshank's warning.'

As the couple made their way to church on the first Sunday after Lammas, the cornfield swayed and beat around them like an angry gleaming ocean. Nine o'clock on an August morning and it was half-dark in the village of Bungay, caught in a noose of the river, fifteen miles from Norwich and fifteen miles from the sea.

'Coming in?' shouted the man to the church warden who was perched up on the roof, cleaning the gutter.

Whatever the warden replied was swept away on the tides of air. The man and his wife couldn't hear a word.

'Old heathen!' the woman said.

Inside the church, it was even darker. In the gloom, the pale faces in their pews shone like anemones. And the wind, wrestling and tugging at the old walls, unable to force its way in, made the stillness in that place seem all the greater – something greater than the gathering storm and yet something you could almost reach out to and touch.

The man and his wife and all the villagers, gathered to hear divine service and common prayer, listened to the stillness, and the mounting wind, and the tolling bell.

'Let us pray,' said the priest.

There was a flash of lightning then. Every window in the church flickered and danced and for a moment the aisle shone brilliantly with a freezing light. The thunder followed before the man and his wife had time even to look at each other: a fearful crack, then a long-drawn roll leaving them, becoming more and more distant, until it seemed only to be its own echo. After that came the rain, tapping, rapping, increasing so that the whole roof over their heads seemed to be one throbbing pulse.

'Let us pray,' called the priest.

There was a rustling. Inside the church, it was as dark now as a cloudless night. The priest could not see his congregation, the man and his wife could not even see beyond their own noses.

'The corn,' muttered the man. 'It'll flatten the corn.'

'What have we done wrong?' said his wife, clutching her husband's arm. 'What wrong have we done?'

Such was the fury of the storm that there was no one in that building who was not afraid for his life.

Then the lightning struck again. Its aim was accurate. Men and women screamed and thought they had come to the end of the world. In the dazzling light, a huge black dog leaped out from the altar and raced down the length of the church. The church quaked and staggered, and the kneeling villagers dived to left and right, burying their heads in their arms. And so they remained, crying and clutching, heaped in scrums higgledy-piggledy, while the thunder smashed into their skulls and roared inside them. They were their own gongs. Then the vibrations began to withdraw, to fall away, until the villagers were aware of their own bodies again, prostrate, fallen sideways, and shaking.

The man opened his eyes and saw that the worst of the darkness was passing; the light in the church was like the first light of dawn. He clambered to his feet, and then peered at the old man motionless in the pew in front of him.

'Look!' he heard himself say. 'Look!'

The old man was still kneeling, as if in prayer – and it was exactly the same with the old woman in the pew opposite. But the heads of them both were lolling sideways. Their eyes were open and their necks were broken; both were stone dead.

Then the man and his wife were caught up in the commotion behind them. A group of villagers were gathering around a young lad. Two of them gently lifted him and laid him face down on a pew.

'I saw it,' said the priest. 'As the dog raced down the aisle, it sprang at him. With one claw, it gouged his back.'

The lad was unconscious because of the pain. And while the villagers were still grouped around him, the church door swung open. Everyone turned and jumped. It was the church warden. 'The thunder,' he said. 'It threw me off the roof.'

'The dog,' said the voices out of the gloom. 'That was the dog.'

'My elbows!' said the warden. 'Especially my shoulders!'

'What an escape,' said the man.

'My knees!' said the warden.

'You old heathen,' said the woman. 'That devil of a dog recognised you and spared you!'

'Look here . . .' said the voices.

'And here . . . and here . . .' said the voices.

Then the warden saw the old man and the old woman, their necks wrung like chickens, and the young lad with a gouged back. He fell silent.

When at last the congregation made a move out of the church, they saw the black dog had also savaged the church door and porch with his claws. Neither human flesh nor solid oak nor blocks of limestone had been able to withstand him.

And, once they were outside, they saw the face of the church clock was black, and that it no longer had hands. The warden climbed up to it and looked out and shouted down, 'The wires! The wheels! They're all twisted and torn and broken into pieces.'

The villagers of Bungay looked after the lad like a talisman. They dressed his deep wound, and bandaged it, and plied him with meat and drink. But although he survived, his working days were done. As his wound closed up, he shrank and shrivelled like a piece of leather, scorched by hot fire, or like the mouth of a purse or a bag, drawn together by string.

News of the black dog spread far and wide. And for as long as the young lad lived, people came to Bungay to see him and to talk to him. Long after he had died, they came to see the church clock. And when that was mended, they came, as they still come, to see the claw marks on the door and in the porch.

'That's not the first time men have seen the black dog,' said the man.

'No,' said his wife. 'And that won't be the last.'

Yallery Brown

IT WAS A Sunday night in July and Tom was in no hurry to get back to High Farm. He didn't like hard work and nothing but hard work awaited him – another week of grooming the horses, mucking out the stables, doing odd jobs at all hours around the farm.

Tom took the long way back to the farm from his parents' home. He wandered along the path that led across the west field; it led towards the dark spinney that some people said was haunted. Tom was happy to be out in the moonlight, out in the middle of the broad silent fields and the smell of growing things. It was warm and still and the air was full of little sounds, as though the trees and grass were whispering to themselves.

Then, all at once, Tom heard a kind of sobbing somewhere ahead of him in the darkness. He stopped and listened and thought it was the saddest sound he had ever heard – like a little child scared and exhausted and almost heartbroken. The sob-sobbing lapsed into a moan and then it rose again into a long, whimpering wail. Tom began to peer about in the darkness. He searched everywhere, but though he looked and looked, he could see nothing. The sound was so close, at his very ear, spent and sorrowful, that he called out over and again, 'Whisht, child, whisht! I'll take you back to your mother if you'll only hush now.'

Tom searched under the hedge that ran along the edge of the spinney. Then he scrambled over it and searched along the other side. He searched among the trees in the spinney itself. Then he waded through the long grass and weeds, but he only frightened some sleeping birds, and stung his hands on a bunch of nettles.

Tom stopped and scratched his head, and felt like giving up. But then, in the quietness, the whimpering became louder and stronger, and Tom thought he could hear words of some sort. He strained his ears and, mixed up with the sobbing, he made out the words, 'Oh! Oh! The great big stone! Ooh! Ooh! The stone on top!'

Tom started to search again. In the dark, he peered here and peered there and at last, down by the far end of the hedge, almost buried in the earth and hidden amongst the matted grass and weeds, he found a great flat stone.

'A Strangers' Table,' said Tom to himself, and he felt uneasy at the thought of meddling with it. He didn't want to cross the little people and bring ill luck on his head by disturbing their moonlight dancing-floor. All the same, he did get down on his knees and put an ear to the stone.

At once he heard it clearer than ever, a weary little voice sobbing, 'Ooh! Ooh! The stone, the stone on top!'

Uneasy as he was about touching the thing, Tom couldn't bear the sound of the little child trapped under it. He tore like mad at the stone until he felt it begin to shift and lift from the earth. Then, with a sigh, the great slab suddenly came away, out of the damp soil and tangled grass and growing things. And there, in the hollow, was a little creature lying on his back, blinking up at the moon and at Tom.

He was no bigger than a year-old baby but he had long tangled hair and a long beard wound round and round his body so that Tom couldn't even see his clothes. His hair, like a baby's hair, was all yellow and shining and silken; but one look at his face and you would have thought he had lived for hundreds and hundreds of years – it was just a heap of wrinkles, with two shining black eyes, surrounded by masses of shining yellow hair. The creature's skin was the colour of freshly-turned earth in the spring, as brown as brown could be; and his hands and feet were just as brown as his face.

He had stopped moaning now but the tears still shone on his cheeks. He looked quite dazed by the moonlight and the night air.

While Tom wondered what to do, the creature suddenly scrambled out of the hollow and stood up and began to look around him. He didn't reach up to Tom's knee and Tom thought he was the strangest thing he had ever set eyes on: brown and yellow all over, yellow and brown, with such a glint in his eyes, and such a wizened face, that Tom felt afraid of him for all that he was so little and so old.

In a while, the creature got used to the moonlight. Then he looked up and boldly stared Tom in the eye. 'Tom,' he said, as cool as you like, 'you're a good lad.' His voice was soft and high and piping like a bird and he said it a second time. 'Tom, you're a good lad.'

Tom pulled at his cap and wondered what to reply. But he was so scared that his jaw seemed locked; he couldn't open his mouth.

'Houts!' said the creature. 'You needn't be afraid of me. You've done me a better turn than you know, my lad, and I'll do the same for you.'

Tom was still too scared to reply but he thought to himself, 'Lord, he's a bogle, and no mistake!'

'No,' said the creature, quick as quick. 'I'm not a bogle, but you'd do better not to ask me what I am. Anyway, I'm a good friend of yours.'

Tom's knees knocked together when the creature said that. He knew no ordinary being could read thoughts. But still, the creature seemed so friendly and reasonable that, in a quavery voice, he managed to say, 'May I be asking your honour's name?'

'H'm,' said the creature, and he pulled his beard. 'As for that . . .' and he thought for a moment. 'As for that, yes, Yallery Brown you can call me. Yallery Brown. That's what I am, and it'll do as well as any other name. Yallery Brown, Tom; Yallery Brown is your friend, my lad.'

'Thank you, master,' said Tom meekly.

'And now,' said the creature, 'I'm in a hurry tonight, but tell me quickly, what shall I do for you? Do you want a wife? I can give you the prettiest girl in town. Do you want to be rich? I'll give you as much gold as you can carry. Or do you want help with your work? Only say the word.'

Tom scratched his head. 'Well,' he said, 'as for a wife, I've no wish to get married; wives spell nothing but trouble, and I've got a mother and sister to mend my clothes. And as for gold, that's as maybe. . . .' Tom grinned and thought that the creature was boasting and couldn't do as much as he had offered. 'But work,' said

Tom. 'There! I can't stand work and if you'll give me a helping hand I'll thank . . .'

'Stop!' said the creature, quick as lightning. 'I'll help you and you're welcome. But if ever you say that word to me – if ever you *thank* me – you'll never see me again. Beware! I want no thanks and I'll have no thanks, do you hear me?' Yallery Brown stamped one little foot on the ground and looked as wicked as a raging bull.

'Mind that, now, you great lump!' said Yallery Brown, calming down a bit. 'And if ever you need help, or get into trouble, just call for me and say, 'Yallery Brown, come from the earth, Yallery Brown, I want you.' Just call for me and I'll be at your side at once.

'And now,' said Yallery Brown, picking a dandelion puff, 'good night to you.' And he blew the dandelion seed into Tom's eyes and ears. When Tom could see again, the little creature had disappeared; and but for the uprooted stone and hollow at his feet, Tom would have thought he had been dreaming.

Then Tom went back home instead of going up to High Farm, and went to bed; and in the morning he had almost forgotten about Yallery Brown. But when he did go up to work at the farm there was nothing to do! It was all done already: the horses were groomed, the stables were mucked out, everything was neat and tidy, and Tom had nothing to do but sit around with his hands in his pockets.

It was just the same the next day, and the day after. All Tom's work was done by Yallery Brown, and done better than Tom could have done it himself. And if the farmer gave Tom more work, Tom simply sat down and watched the work get done by itself. The singeing irons and the besom and this, that and the other all set to and got through their tasks in no time. For Tom never saw Yallery Brown out in the light of day; it was only in the darkness that he saw him hopping about, like a will-o'-the-wyke without his lantern.

To begin with, Tom couldn't have been happier. He had nothing to do, and got well paid for it! But after a time, things began to go wrong. Not only was Tom's work done but the work of the other farmhands was undone: if his buckets were filled, theirs were upset; if his tools were sharpened, theirs were blunted and wrecked; if his horses were clean as daisies, theirs were splashed with muck. That's how things were, day in and day out, always the same.

The other farmhands saw Yallery Brown flitting around night after night; they saw things that worked without helping hands; and they saw that Tom's work was done for him, and their work was undone for them. Naturally they began to fight shy of Tom. After a while, they wouldn't speak to him or even go near him. And, in the end, they all went to the farmer and told him what was happening.

Tom often thought he would be better off doing his own work after all, and wished that Yallery Brown would leave him and his old friends in peace. But he was utterly unable to do anything about it – brooms wouldn't so much as stay in his hand, the plough ran away from him, the hoe kept slipping out of his grip. He could only sit on his own, while all the other lads gave him the cold shoulder and Yallery Brown worked for him and worked against all the others.

At last, things got so bad that the farmer gave Tom the sack; and if he hadn't, all the other farmhands would probably have sacked the farmer, for they vowed they would no longer stay on the same farm with Tom.

Tom was angry and upset then. It was a very good farm, and he was well paid; he was hopping mad with Yallery Brown for getting him into such trouble. And, without thinking, he shook his fist and shouted as loud as he could, 'Yallery Brown, come out of the earth; Yallery Brown, you scamp, I want you.'

Tom had done no more than close his mouth when he felt something tweaking the back of his leg. It pinched him and he jumped, and when he looked down, Tom could scarcely believe his eyes – for there already was the little creature with his shining hair and wrinkled face and wickedly glinting black eyes.

Tom was in a fine old rage and he would have liked nothing so much as to give Yallery Brown a big kick, but the creature was so small he would only have slid off the side of his boot. Tom scowled and said, 'Look here, master, I'll thank you to leave me alone from now on, do you hear me? I want none of your help, and I'll have nothing more to do with you. Understand?'

The horrid little creature gave a screech of a laugh and pointed a brown finger at Tom. 'Ho, ho, Tom!' he said. 'You've just thanked me, my lad, and I told you not to, I told you not to!'

'I don't want any of your help, I tell you,' yelled Tom. 'I only want never to see you again, and to have nothing more to do with you.'

The more Tom said, the more Yallery Brown laughed and screeched and mocked. 'Tom, my lad,' he said with a devilish grin, 'I'll tell you something, Tom. It's true enough I'll never help you again, and call on me as you will, you'll never see me again after today.'

'Good,' said Tom.

'But I never said I'd leave you alone, Tom, and I never will, my lad! I was nice and safe under that stone, Tom, and I could do no harm. But you let me out yourself, and you can't put me back again.'

Tom grimaced and shook his head.

'I would have been your friend,' said Yallery Brown, 'and worked for you if you had been wise; but since you're a born fool, I'll give you nothing but fool's luck. When everything goes wrong and arsy-versy, you'll know it's Yallery Brown's doing, even if you can't see him. Mark my words, Tom!'

And Yallery Brown began to dance round Tom, looking like a little child with all his yellow hair, but looking older than ever with his grinning wrinkled face. And as he danced, he sang:

> *Work as you will*
> *You'll never do well;*
> *Work as you may,*
> *You'll never make hay;*
> *For harm and bad luck and Yallery Brown*
> *You've let out yourself from under the stone.*

The words rang in Tom's ears over and again. Then Yallery Brown just stood there, mocking, and grinning at Tom, and chuckling as wickedly as the devil himself.

Tom was terrified. He could only stand there, shaking all over, staring down at the horrible little creature.

Then Yallery Brown's shining yellow hair lifted and rippled in a gust of wind. It wound round and round him so that he looked for all the world like a great dandelion puff. And then the little creature floated away on the breeze over the wall and out of sight; as he went,

Tom could hear the last skirl of an insult and a sneering laugh.

Tom was scared to death and, after that day, his fortunes took a tumble. He worked here and worked there, he put his hand to this and that, but something always went wrong.

The years passed by and Tom married and had children. But his children died and his wife didn't – when she scolded him, people could hear her a mile off, and Tom thought now and then that he could have spared *her*! And although he tried his hand with cattle and sheep and pigs and goats and hens, none of them fattened as they should. Nothing ever worked for him.

No, Tom had no luck at all after meeting Yallery Brown. For the rest of his life, until he was dead and buried and maybe afterwards, there was no end to Yallery Brown's spite towards him. And day after day as long as he lived, even as an old man when he sat trembling beside the fire, Tom heard a voice singing:

> *Work as you will*
> *You'll never do well;*
> *Work as you may,*
> *You'll never make hay;*
> *For harm and bad luck and Yallery Brown*
> *You've let out yourself from under the stone.*

The Green Children

·····———◆———·····

CLAC straightened his back, braced his aching shoulders, and grunted. Sweat trickled down his face and dripped from the end of his nose. He licked his lips; they tasted of salt. Clac glanced down the long, straight swaths of corn; then, rubbing the back of his neck between his shoulder blades, he considered the position of the sun. But his stomach was his best clock. He filled his lungs, cupped a huge hand to his mouth, and bellowed 'FOOD'.

The other cottars heard him. One by one they stopped work and mopped their brows; one by one they left their own strips of land and began to walk slowly towards him.

Their scythes gleamed in the midday sun; a very small wind moved over the swathes and whispered warnings to the ears of uncut corn.

'Come on,' called Clac. He sat on the turf balk dividing his strip from the next, waiting impatiently. 'This sun . . . I've had enough of it.'

'So have I,' sighed Swein, collapsing in a heap like a sack of potatoes.

'Come on,' cried Clac. 'You and you and all the rest of you.' He picked up a flitch with one hand and with the other a gourd of cider. 'I'm for the shade. Shade first, then food. Who'll carry the apples?'

'I will,' said Grim.

So the cottars, nine of them in all, set off across the common land, on which their cattle grazed. They walked towards the Wolfpits – where, in winter, wild creatures roamed – and towards the high, waving elms.

Clac led the way. He always did; he liked leading. And the lord of the manor, Sir Richard de Caine, who had recognised this quality in him, had put him over the other cottars and villeins. As the tired, hungry men approached the elms, Clac stopped in his tracks. 'Look!'

'What?' said Grim.

'Where?' said Swein.

'Look!' Clac exclaimed again. 'Look! There!' He pointed towards the trees. 'Follow me.' And throwing down the flitch and the gourd, he started to run. He ran and ran until at last he came to the old wolfpits just beyond the elms.

'Look!' insisted Clac, pointing again. 'Look!'

And there, huddling in the hollow of the largest pit, the cottars saw what Clac had seen: two green children. Their skin was green, their hair was green, they wore green clothes. And one was a boy, the other was a girl.

For a moment, nobody moved, nobody spoke. The cottars looked down at the green children and the green children looked up at the cottars.

'Blessed Edmund preserve us!' exclaimed Clac. And he made the sign of the cross.

'And St William of Norwich,' muttered Grim. And he crossed himself too.

'Who can they be?' said Swein helplessly.

'Ask them.' said Clac.

Swein laughed nervously.

'All right then,' said Clac. 'I will. I'll ask them.' But he was nervous too; the break in his voice betrayed him.

The cottars bunched together anxiously.

'They might be little folk,' Swein warned him.

'Let's leave them alone,' said Thurketil.

'Look at them,' Clac replied. 'Do they look as if they mean harm?'

The cottars crowded round the edge of the pit, watching breathlessly. If one man had moved, the rest would have toppled headlong down. The boy and the girl were clutching one another, looking up at the nine men fearfully. And then, quite unexpectedly, the green girl buried her face in her hands and began to sob.

'You see?' said Clac. He stepped forward, slipped down the grassy bank, and walked towards the children.

The closer he drew, the more astonished he became – so much so that he completely forgot his nervousness. In all this thirty years, he had never seen or even heard of anything like it before: green children . . . a boy and a girl with green cheeks, green fingers, and, poking out of their green sandals, green toes.

'Hallo!' said Clac in his gruff, friendly voice. 'Who are you?' And he smiled encouragingly.

The children huddled still closer together. They gazed at Clac, bewildered, and said nothing.

Clac looked at the children closely. He saw that they resembled each other not only because they were green, but also in the mould of their features. 'You must be brother and sister,' he said. He was right.

Clac also guessed that the girl was about nine and that the boy was about seven.

'Who are you?' he repeated. 'Where do you come from?'

The children continued to gaze at him silently.

'Well,' thought Clac. 'It's clear enough: either they're dumb or they don't understand me.'

At this moment the boy turned to the girl and spoke several strange words.

'That settles it,' said Clac. 'You don't understand me. . . And I can't pretend to understand you.'

The green girl looked at Clac; suddenly, she flashed a smile at him, opened her mouth and pointed at it.

'Blessed Edmund preserve me!' exclaimed Clac. 'She's got a green tongue.' He nodded and grinned. 'I see,' he said. 'You're hungry.'

He turned round, waved reassuringly to the other cottars, and called, 'What are you doing up there, you idlers? Get the flitch and bring it down. And bring the cider too.'

In no time, the cottars were pouring down into the pit, bringing the food with them. They swarmed round the children, their superstition at last overcome by curiosity.

'Here! Give me the flitch,' said Clac.

Swein passed it to him.

Clac sniffed at it, then showed it to the two children.

They looked at it blankly, then turned to each other and shook their heads. Then the girl sniffed it, and wrinkled up her nose.

'Look at that!' marvelled Clac. 'They've never seen a flitch before.'

Now it was his turn to shake his head. 'What about the apples, then?' he said. 'Give me two red apples.'

'Here,' said Grim, and passed them over.

The two children looked at them, turned to each other again, and shook their heads a second time.

Clac was dumbfounded. He didn't know what to do . . . but he didn't like to admit it. 'How about that?' he asked. 'How about that? They've never seen apples before.'

Despite their behaviour, it was clear that the two children were famished. Again and again they pointed to their mouths. And once more the green girl began to weep.

'I . . . hm . . . I think we should take them to Sir Richard,' said Clac. The other cottars nodded in agreement.

'Sir Richard's a traveller,' Clac continued. 'He's travelled far and wide, almost as far as the edges of the earth. Perhaps he's heard of green children.'

So the cottars escorted the green children to the manor of Sir Richard de Caine. And as they walked, they sang, for they were not altogether sorry to miss an afternoon's work under the blazing sun. But the children were dazzled by the bright light. They kept their heads down, and shielded their eyes with their arms.

The fortified manor was surrounded by a moat. Clac strode to the brink, and shouted to the guards on the other side. For a while the guards conferred, then they let the drawbridge down. The little group, with the children in their midst, walked across and on into the great hall.

'Wait here!' said a guard, his eyes bulging out of his head as he looked at the two children. 'Until Sir Richard comes.'

Inside the hall, out of the sunlight, the children looked about them with great curiosity. They ran to and fro, exclaiming in wonder at the huge stone fireplace, the narrow windowslits, the yellow rushes on the floor. They chattered excitedly, and for a moment even forgot their hunger.

*　　*　　*

'Green children,' boomed a voice at the entrance of the hall. 'What's all this?'

The cottars swung round.

And there, hands on hips, stood Sir Richard de Caine, an enormous, pot-bellied man.

The cottars liked him well. He was a just lord, and a generous one, though his moods were as variable as the weather: one day he was laughing and smiling, the next thundering commands to his frightened servants.

But now he was completely silent. He was staring at the green children open-mouthed.

'Please my lord,' said Clac, stepping forward. And he explained to Sir Richard how he had discovered the green children at the Wolfpits. 'And they don't speak English,' he said, 'and they won't eat our food.'

From his great height, Sir Richard looked down at the shrinking children. He frowned and stroked his beard.

Sir Richard liked problems; he enjoyed solving them. But green children, green as grass, who couldn't speak English, who wouldn't eat apples . . . that was another thing altogether.

'So they don't speak English,' echoed Sir Richard after a long pause. 'Ah well! I don't blame them. Perhaps they speak Norman.' He stooped, smiled warmly at the green girl, and began, 'D'ou venez-vous?'

The green girl gazed at him blankly. Then she looked to her brother; he shrugged his shoulders, and repeated the strange words that Clac had heard in the Wolfpits. Whereupon the girl looked up at Sir Richard, pointed at his pot-belly and opened her mouth.

Sir Richard bellowed with laughter. 'I understand you,' he cried. 'Food's a common language. All right. Sit them down.' Then, walking to the entrance of the hall, he shouted at the top of his voice, 'FOOD, FOOD.'

Clac led the two children over to the trestle table and sat them at the wooden bench.

In no time, a servant bustled in, bearing part of a chicken on a platter; a second followed, carrying a bunch of succulent, black grapes; and the third brought a pitcher of red wine. 'Give them each a wing,' said Sir Richard. 'That'll tempt them. You see if it doesn't.'

But the children pushed the chicken away, indicating that they would not eat it.

'What about the grapes, then?' suggested Sir Richard.

The black, succulent grapes were set before them. The girl fingered one and said something to her brother. Then they refused them too.

Sir Richard strode up and down the hall, disconcerted. 'Bring them some cheese, then,' he instructed.

A servant hurried out of the hall, reappeared with a bowl of cream cheese, and placed it on the table.

The two children took one look at it and pushed that away too.

'Well!' exclaimed Sir Richard. 'I don't know. What *will* they eat?'

At this moment, it so happened that an old servant was crossing the far end of the hall. In his arms, he carried a pile of freshly cut beans, still attached to their stalks.

Seeing the beans, the green children cried out with delight. They leaped up from the bench and ran toward the old man who was so startled at the sight of them that he threw down the beans on the spot and ran out of the hall as fast as his old legs could carry him.

The children fell upon the pile and immediately began to tear open the stalks, thinking the beans were in the hollows of them. Finding none, they were utterly dismayed and began to weep dismally once more.

'Look!' said Clac. 'Like this.' He quickly opened a pod and showed them the naked beans.

And so at last the green children began to eat.

The cottars stood watching them.

'I see,' said Richard eventually. 'I see. Green children, green food.'

After they had eaten their fill, the green children smiled gratefully at Sir Richard de Caine and the cottars.

'Well! Now what?' said Sir Richard. 'What are we going to do with them now?'

This was a question no one could answer. And as the two children showed no inclination to leave the hall, Sir Richard instructed that they should be allowed to remain at the manor for as long as they desired. He asked his priest, Father John, to teach them to speak English.

And for many, many months the green children ate nothing but beans.

The great fair at Stourbridge came and went. Sir Richard de Caine journeyed there, laden with packs of wool, and returned with Baltic furs, French cloth and lace, and salts and spices from the East. And all this time the green children stayed at the manor. Father John took his duties seriously; each day the children had English lessons with him. They both worked hard and made good progress.

And the old priest, a lean, angular man who often declared he loved no one but God, began to love the green boy and the green girl as if they were his own children.

'They must be baptised,' he told Sir Richard one day. 'They may be green but they still have souls.'

And so the children were baptised. The ceremony was attended by Sir Richard de Caine and by all his household, and by his cottars and villeins.

August grew old; September was born. High winds wrestled with the sun. Leaves fell, carpeting the earth in copper and bronze and gold. The elms by the Wolfpits looked like skeletons.

Clac and his fellow cottars brought the harvest home and began to prepare for winter. They killed pigs and cattle and fowls, and gave them to their wives who cut them up, and salted them, and stored them away for harder days.

During the cold days of November, the green boy became listless. He would eat no more beans; he made little progress in his work; he lost interest in playing draughts and spinning tops; and nothing his sister said could cheer him.

Nobody could say what was wrong with him; he ran no fever, sported no spots. And his sister could speak so little English she was unable to explain. . . .

Father John was anxious. He made the green boy eat mugwort and mayweed, crab-apple, thyme and fennel; he sent to Bury for water from the Well of Our Lady; he offered prayers.

It was all to no avail. One dark day, when the ground was like iron underfoot and the shifting skies were grey, the green boy threw up his hands and died.

Throughout the long hard winter his sister could not be consoled. Often she wept; it was so cold the tears froze on her cheeks. But at last, as spring threw off winter, she too threw off her grief. The crocuses flowered.

One evening Sir Richard de Caine and his family, his servants and guards, and all the cottars and villeins who worked on his demesne, gathered in the great hall.

First the company ate. The food was drawn from earth and air and sea. There was crane and swan, peacock and snipe; there was sucking-pig and, out of season, venison; there were lampreys, sea-trout and sturgeon. And to wash down this sumptuous fare, there was spiced wine.

After the meal it was customary for the minstrel to sing. The company turned from the tables to face the minstrel and the fire.

'Not tonight,' called Sir Richard. 'We'll not have songs tonight. I've asked you all for a special reason.' He paused and looked round the hall. 'Our guest,' he continued, and smiling turned to the green girl, 'can speak English at last. She has told me who she is, and where she comes from. And now I have asked her to tell her story to you.'

There was a rustle of excitement.

The green girl stood up and walked over to the minstrel's place beside the flickering fire. Her shadow danced on the wall behind her. All at once she smiled, the same alluring smile she had first flashed at Clac in the Wolfpits. Then she began in a strong, clear voice, 'I come from a green country. The people are green, the animals are green, the earth and sky are green. There is nothing that is not green.

'The sun never shines in my country. The light there is a constant green glow, as if the sun was always just below the horizon.'

A puff of woodsmoke filled the room. The listeners coughed and rubbed their smarting eyes, then settled again. They had never heard such a thing in their lives.

'From the hills of our country,' said the girl, 'you can see another, much brighter land – though I have never been there – divided from ours by a broad river.'

'But tell us where your land is,' said Sir Richard, 'and how you got here.'

'Well! One day my brother and I . . . my poor brother who died of homesickness . . . we were tending sheep on the hills, and they began to stray. We followed them and came to the mouth of a cave, a great cave we'd never seen before. The sheep entered the cave and we walked in after them. And there, ahead of us, we heard the sound of bells: a most beautiful sound, loud bells and soft bells, treble bells and bass bells, ringing, ringing.

'It seemed,' said the green girl, 'that the sound came from the far end of the cave. The bells were so beautiful they pulled us towards them. We *had* to find them. So we walked through the cave, on and on. At first it was flat; then we began to climb. And the bells rang and rang, tugging us towards them.

'The cave was gloomy but not dark; then, suddenly, we saw a bright light some way ahead of us. "That's where the bells are coming from," my brother said. So we hurried towards it. It grew and grew, dazzling us. And all at once we climbed up and out, out of the cave,' said the girl. 'The ringing stopped, the sunlight blinded us.' She clapped her hands to her eyes. 'We were knocked senseless by the sun. We lay in a swoon for a long time . . .'

Everyone in the hall was leaning forward. The fire roared.

'When we recovered our senses, we saw we were in some deep pit. And although we looked for the entrance to the cave, it had completely gone; we couldn't find it again. "What shall we do?" my brother asked me. "I don't know," I said. I felt rather afraid. "But as we can't go back, we'd better go forward." So, very cautiously, we climbed out of the Wolfpits . . .'

'That's it,' exclaimed Clac excitedly. 'I remember. That's when I saw you.'

The green girl smiled.

'"Blessed Edmund preserve me," I said,' continued Clac. 'Two green children.'

'If you were surprised to see green children,' the girl replied, 'think how astonished we were to see pink men!'

95

Everyone laughed.

'Not only astonished,' continued the green girl, 'but frightened too. My brother and I backed down into the pit again. But we couldn't find the entrance to the cave; and so you caught us.'

The assembled company sighed, and nodded their heads.

'That's my story,' said the green girl. 'The rest you know. Thank you all for your great kindness to me. I've been very happy here; but if ever I can find the entrance to the cave, I must return home.'

With that, she sat down.

But that was only the beginning. Many were the questions asked of her that night; many were the answers given.

But the years passed and the green girl did not return home. She remained at the manor, for she was unable to find the entrance to the cave.

In time she learned to eat meat, and the fruits of the earth, and even to enjoy them. And slowly her skin lost its green tinge, her hair became fair.

She always said that she was very happy in this world. But often Clac and the cottars saw her wandering down by the Wolfpits, alone. At such times, they never went near her. For they knew that she must be lonely for her own people, and looking for the entrance to the cave.

One spring the green girl married. She left the manor of Sir Richard de Caine and went to live with her husband at Lenna near King's Lynn. But even then she used to return to the Wolfpits from time to time. Her feet were anchored to this earth, but her heart and mind sailed on to another far-off land.

How, then, did it end? What became of the girl who climbed up from the green land?

All this happened years and years ago. Eight hundred years ago. Some things live longer than centuries, others do not. We know much about the green girl, but there is much we do not know.

And nobody knows – unless you do – whether the green girl lived on earth to the end of her days; or whether, one day, near the Wolfpits, she simply disappeared.

Sources

····———◆———····

SOURCES AND NOTES for those who would like to search out the originals, or to visit some of the places and sights mentioned in these tales.

THE DEAD MOON. 'Legends of the Lincolnshire Cars' by Mrs M. C. Balfour in Folk-Lore, Volume II. Folk-Lore Society, London, 1891.

Mrs Balfour says that she heard the story from a girl of nine, a cripple, who had heard it from her grandmother. 'But I think,' she writes, 'it was tinged by her own fancy, which seemed to lean to eerie things, and she certainly revelled in the gruesome descriptions, fairly making my flesh creep with her words and gestures.'

I have kept very close to the original but modified the heavy Lincolnshire dialect.

TOM HICKATHRIFT. *Chap-Books and Folk-Lore Tracts*, No. I, edited by G. L. Gomme and H. B. Wheatley for the Villon Society, London, 1885. This is a reprint of the chapbook in the Pepysian Library at Magdalene College, Cambridge, which was printed sometime between 1660 and 1690.

It seems likely that the hero of this story, which incorporates so many traditional motifs, actually existed (though it is impossible to say precisely when), and there are various traditions associating him with the Tilney villages near King's Lynn.

In the original, the death of the giant is followed by the episodes with the footballers, the thieves and the tinker. Since the killing of the giant forms the climax of the tale I have, like Joseph Jacobs, rearranged the running order.

THE SUFFOLK MIRACLE. *English and Scottish Popular Ballads* edited by F. J. Child, Boston, 1857–9. Child reprinted the ballad from a broadside in the Roxburghe Collection.

The rather sketchy ballad does not really do justice to the Suffolk version of this haunting and widely-known story. Child writes: 'A tale of a dead man coming on horseback to his inconsolable love, and carrying her to his grave, is widely spread among the Slavic people and the Austrian Germans, was well known a century ago among the northern Germans, and has lately been recovered in the Netherlands, Denmark, Iceland and Brittany.'

I have departed from the original in allowing Rosamund to be present when her lover's grave is opened, given names to the protagonists, and generally tried to add a little colour and suspense to the ballad's pace.

THE PEDLAR OF SWAFFHAM. *The Diary of Abraham de la Pryme* edited by Charles Jackson, The Surtees Society, 1870. Reprinted by J. Glyde in *The Norfolk Garland*, London, 1872, which has an additional section about how the first treasure found by John Chapman had a Latin inscription on the lid. The earliest account of this story is to be found in Blomefield's *A Topographical History of the County of Norfolk*, 1739–75.

In 1462, a pedlar (or chapman) paid for the new north aisle of Swaffham Church in Norfolk, and contributed to the cost of the spire. This is recorded in the fifteen-century *Black Book* which is still in Swaffham Church Library, and which includes a list of benefactors to the church. The rebuilding of the church was actually begun in 1452 but not completed until the middle of the sixteenth century. You can see it today; you can see fragments of John Chapman's chair (carved with the figure of a pedlar with a pack on his back and a mastiff at his side) and of the old stained glass (which showed the pedlar with his wife and three children); you can see the spire, a pointed reminder, from miles off.

I have added to the original some details to give a picture of the fifteenth-century journey to London, and to suggest the pedlar's state of mind.

THE GREEN MIST. 'Legends of the Lincolnshire Cars' by Mrs M. C. Balfour in Folk-Lore, Volume II. Folk-Lore Society, London, 1891.

I have introduced into the story itself some of the folk customs alluded to in the source's preamble. I have also converted some of the reported action into direct action, with the use of dialogue, and have attempted a description of the green mist itself. As in the other stories taken from Mrs Balfour, I have modified the Lincolnshire dialect.

THE CALLOW PIT COFFER. *The Norfolk Garland* edited by John Glyde, London, 1872.

Southwood is a little hamlet lying between Norwich and Great Yarmouth. When the Church of St Edmund at Southwood (it was a thatched church) fell into disrepair in 1881, the iron ring from Callow Pit was taken to the neighbouring parish of Limpenhoe and fastened to the church door. It is there now.

I have chosen to set the story in the reign of King Stephen (1135–54) and introduced a supporting cast of villagers.

THE DAUNTLESS GIRL. *The Recreations of a Norfolk Antiquary* by Walter Rye, Norwich, 1920. Reprinted from the Norton Collection (MS. six volumes).

I have kept close to the original, only stopping to modify the dialect and to put a few words into the mouths of the farmer's drinking companions.

TIDDY MUN 'Legends of the Lincolnshire Cars' by Mrs M. C. Balfour, in Folk-Lore, Volume II. Folk-Lore Society, London, 1891.

Tiddy Mun is clearly the spirit of the marshes. Mrs Balfour heard the story from an old woman who had lived all her life in the Cars, 'who in her young days herself observed the rite she describes, though she would not confess to it within the hearing of her grand-children, whose indifference and disbelief shocked her greatly. To her, 'Tiddy Mun' was a perfect reality, and one to be loved as well as feared.'

As with the other stories taken from Mrs Balfour, I have stuck close to the original while modifying the dialect.

THE BLACK DOG OF BUNGAY. *The Table Book of Daily Recreation and Information, and Year Book* by W. Hone, London, 1833. Reprinted by E. S. Hartland (editor) in *County Folk-Lore*, Volume I: Suffolk, Folk-Lore Society, London, 1895.

This event, subtitled 'A Strange and Terrible Wunder', is said to have taken place on Sunday 4th August, 1557, at Holy Trinity Church, Bungay, on the border of Norfolk and Suffolk. One version (the one I have followed) tells of two people being killed and one severely burned while attending morning service; another says that two men were 'Sleyn in the Tempest in the Belfry in Time of Prayer.' The dog was seen on the same day at Blibery Church, seven miles from Bungay, where he killed two men and a boy, and burned the hand of another.

I have introduced the idea of two villagers on their way to church, and dramatised a story which reads in the original like a newspaper report.

YALLERY BROWN. 'Legends of the Lincolnshire Cars' by Mrs M. C. Balfour in Folk-Lore, Volume II, Folk-Lore Society, London, 1891.

This is Yallery Brown's song and why the dialect needs modifying!

Wo'k as thou wull
Thou'll niver do well;
Wo'k as thou mowt
Thou'll niver gain owt;
Fur harm an' mischaunce an' Yallery Brown
Thou's let oot thy-sel' fro' unner th' sto'an.

THE GREEN CHILDREN. *Chronicon Anglicanum* by Ralph of Coggeshall, Rolls Series No. 66 (Rerum Brittanicarum medii aevi scriptores), 1857. Reprinted, Brussels, 1963.

An early eighteenth century historian, William of Newbridge, writing six hundred years after Ralph of Coggeshall, also recorded this story. He said that the green children were found at Woolpit (named after the Wolf Pits) four or five miles from Bury St Edmunds in Suffolk. He also records that the green girl said that her country was called St Martin's Land, because that saint was worshipped there, and that the people there were Christians.

William of Newbridge set the story in the reign of King Stephen (1135–54) and that is where I have set it too. But the idea of little people coming up out of the earth is far older than that. It is age-old, but each age claims it as its own.

Glossary

archery butts	A mark or target for archery practice. By law every male peasant had to possess a longbow and arrows and practise regularly at the butts.
balk	a ridge
boggart, bogle	both are kinds of bogie, which is the name for a wide range of spirits who mislead human beings. Boggarts are, on the whole, no worse than mischievous while bogles can be frightening and dangerous.
chapman	a pedlar. People were often called by their professions: for instance, Butcher, Cooper, Taylor, Smith.
the Chronicle	the Anglo-Saxon Chronicle, a year by year history of England inspired by King Alfred and continued up to 1154, the end of the reign of King Stephen
clappers	castanets
cottar	a peasant, a cottager who owned an acre or two of his own but had to do a certain amount of work on his lord's land.
demesne	estate, land
Edmund	a ninth-century King of the East Anglians and once the patron saint of England. He was killed by the Danes in 869.

flitch	a 'side' of bacon, salted and cured.
the Gold Road	a road from Lynn, the major port in Norfolk, to London. It was so called because of the stream of valuable exports and imports carried along it.
gourd	a drinking bottle made from the hollowed shell of the gourd fruit.
humstrum	a one-stringed roughly-made musical instrument.
Lammas Day	August 1st.
mastiff	a powerful dog with a large head, drooping ears and pendulous lips.
mothering cakes	cakes eaten on Mothering Sunday, which falls in the middle of Lent.
mugwort, mayweed, crab-apple, thyme, fennel	different herbs, used as medicines.
open fields	the arable land of an ordinary village, cultivated in two great open fields which were divided into strips belonging to the cottars and their lord.
pardoner	a man authorised by the Pope to forgive sins in return for money. As often as not pardoners were rascals, and thieved from the poor.
portmanteau	a case or bag, usually made of leather, for carrying money, clothing and other necessaries.
ramping	high-spirited, leaping, gallivanting.
Saint Swithin's Day	July 15th. The saying is: 'If it rains on St Swithin's day, there will be rain for forty days.'

shoot the bridge	the water passed very swiftly under London Bridge. So boats 'shot the bridge' as, today, boats, 'shoot the falls'.
sillier	more helpless, more frail, more sickly.
Southwood	a village that lies several miles to the south of the Norwich–Yarmouth road; the nearest town is Acle.
the Spon	a boggy place
Stephen de Blois	King of England, 1135–54
sulphurous mist	traditionally regarded as hellish
swath	a line of reaped corn.
the Three Cranes	a hostelry in Upper Thames Street. Passengers landed there and rejoined their boat at Billingsgate (or vice versa) for fear of an upset in the turbulent water under the bridge.
villein	a peasant of lower class than the cottar, obliged to do a large amount of work on his lord's land.
wattle and daub	rods or stakes, interlaced with twigs, used to make a framework for walls. This was covered with daub which was a brittle plaster made of a mixture of dung and mud and straw.
will-o'-the-wykes	also called *will-o'-the-wisp*. In the Lincolnshire fens, it is a spirit, often an evil one, carrying a flickering lantern.